THAUMATURGIC TAPAS

A HIDDEN DISHES NOVELLA

TAO WONG

Thaumaturgic Tapas

A Starlit Publishing Book
Published by Starlit Publishing

PO Box 30035
High Park PO
Toronto, ON
M6P 3K0
Canada

www.starlitpublishing.com

Ebook ISBN: 9781778551963

Paperback ISBN: 9781778551970

Contents

1. Mung Bean Juice   1

2. Morning Preparations   7

3. French Onion Soup   14

4. Extra Hands   20

5. Leftover Vegetables   28

6. Spring Rolls   34

7. Opening Hour   41

8. By the Prickling of my Thumbs   50

9. Orange and Assorted Fruit Kefir   56

10. It's Getting Warm in Here   60

11. French Onion Soup (2)   64

12. Stir the Pot, Full of Trouble   73

13. Parboiled, Smashed Garlic Baked   77
     Potatoes

14. Making Do with Others   85

15. The Dirty Past   94

16. Rising to the Challenge   104

17. Battling Chaos   115

18. Drugs and Other Protection   122

19. Bacon Wrapped Anything   129

20. Simple Salads   137

21. Crunch and Crackle   144

22. Making Friends   153

23. Joys of Experimentation   160

24. Final Numbers   170

Author's Note   181

About the Author   183

About the Publisher   185

ONE
Mung Bean Juice

There was something peaceful about the restaurant when it was closed and all the customers were gone. The lights had dimmed, not so much that it was impossible to read like some of the trendier restaurants, but enough that the yellow light created a sense of warmth. The lingering smells of tonight's specials were drifting away, pulled away by the continuing hum of the air circulation system and what Kelly assumed was more magic.

With the guests gone and the chairs up, the floor swept clean and only the muted clatter of dishes being cleared and put away, she found herself relaxing for the first time in hours. She pulled out the single stool that was secreted under the bar, slumping on the pass and staring through it as her boss worked industriously in his domain.

There was a subtle rhythm to his movements, like a dancer twirling through a long-memorized routine but with the very same intensity and focus as they'd have on a performance night. This was no rote movement, as soon forgotten as complete, but the focused attention of the moment, where each –action—from sweeping half-finished meals into the garbage to rinsing the plates off before throwing them into the industrial –dishwasher—was taken with the proper care and reverence of existence.

Only when the dishwasher was filled and set running, another larger stack waiting to go in, did Mo Meng stop. He raised a hand, sweeping a stray black lock out of his face as he walked over to Kelly who'd been staring blankly at him for the last five minutes, exhaustion muddying her thoughts.

The proprietor of the Nameless Restaurant was short for a modern man, but he carried himself with the assurance gained from numerous years on this earth. As though nothing in this world could faze him, not anymore, the rock of his personality was unyielding to the tempest of emotions. Even so, there was always a small smile, a trace of good humor lurking in his eyes.

"Are you okay?" Mo Meng asked, his voice cultured and gentle. His accent was hard to place, most recently Canadian, but also muddied from travel and time.

"Tired." Kelly rubbed her face. "Tonight was rough."

"They won't be back," Mo Meng said, confidently. "Nor will we be serving anyone else who feels the need to raise their voice and shout when they're asked to wait."

"Good," Kelly said. The entire incident, brought about by the long wait times and their refusal to take reservations, had been stressful. There was something about men in expensive suits who felt their time and needs, somehow, were more important than anyone else's. "But it wasn't just them. Dealing with the crowd put me behind. And then the toilet got backed up, and we had to deal with that," thankfully, Mo Meng had stepped in there, "and then the machine went down and we had those two extra tables lingering and the desserts took longer and..."

"And once you got behind, you couldn't get caught up," Mo Meng finished. He made a small noise in his throat before he gestured to the cash register. "Finish up the numbers. I'll be back, and we'll finish this talk."

Humming to himself, he stepped away, turning a burner back on, and placed a fresh pot of water on it. Kelly hesitated, surprised by his sudden disappearance, before giving herself a little shake and moving over to the machine to finish the math. As hard as she worked, there was one advantage to working at the Nameless Restaurant; the patrons tipped well.

If strangely.

Holding the flower in one hand, she reached under the bar and filled a vase with water before placing the flower in it. Golden petals, a darker center, a single straight stem with a pair of leaves on the side. She could not help but sniff at the scent, for a moment taken away to green pastures and warm spring rather than dreary, chilly late winter.

Then she continued counting, doing the math necessary to balance the books and work out her tips. No new-fangled machine here, nothing connected to the internet. Mo Meng categorically refused to bring one of those in here, muttering about spies when asked.

A glance back saw Mo Meng throwing a handful of tiny beans in the boiling pot of water before she returned her attention to her work. Much faster than she had expected, in minutes, he was back, a glass of lukewarm juice in his hand, a mild astringent scent rising from the glass and a trio of ice cubes melting. A single glass straw stood out, waiting for her.

"What is it?" she asked, curiously. It didn't, of course, stop her from tasting the drink.

Surprising, that it wasn't an explosion of taste. In fact it was rather bland, just a hint of boiled beans and a touch of sugar, lukewarm so that it was a warm hug in her mouth. The glass straw warmed a little under her lips, the thin glass delicate between her teeth. Tired as she was, and thirsty, she finished half the glass before she stopped.

"Mung bean water," Mo Meng said. "Boil the mung beans for a few minutes, extract and filter the water, add a little rock sugar and cool. It's nothing special, but it helps with stress and overheating." He nodded at her flushed cheeks.

"That... thank you." She bit off her other thoughts, that no matter how effectively this might alleviate her stress now, it didn't fix the root problem.

"We need more people," Mo Meng said, as if he could read her thoughts. Or perhaps he had just been thinking the same thing. "One at the minimum, but preferably two." He grimaced. "The hours have been getting long, even for me."

"Another waitress, or a busboy and host, yes," she replied. "You need help within too."

It was unclear if his answering grunt was agreement or displeasure or just acknowledgement of her words. Turning back around, he looked at the kitchen, eyes drifting over the boards and bins stacked with uncooked ingredients, to prepped basics and the still-dirty pots, before he came to a conclusion.

"Make a post. Tomorrow, we'll have limited seating. Small dishes, maybe not enough for a meal." A slight chuckle. "Best be here early, if they want to eat at all."

"We're going exclusive?" Now she was surprised, knowing how much he'd resisted that.

"For tomorrow at least. I've got a lot of leftovers to get rid of, ingredients I've prepped too much of, other items that weren't finished up. It'll be a day of getting rid of extras." He nodded to the glass, adding, "There's more if you want it. But get your work done, I'll sign off. And look into hiring."

His part said, he turned and disappeared into the kitchen, grabbing a cloth as he went to begin wiping down dirty surfaces. It left Kelly wondering what was coming to the restaurant, tomorrow and as they hired someone new.

Two
Morning Preparations

He ran a hand through his hair one last time. Trying to get it to stay down with just hard water and a touch of exertion rather than hair grease or soap was futile. Eventually, Mo Meng gave up, his fingers twitching as he considered magicking it flat. He knew a number of cantrips, but it was a good lesson to relearn. Proper care taken –beforehand—in this case, drying his hair –properly—led to better results. Like not looking like a bedraggled human rooster.

Chuckling to himself, he slipped out of the small bathroom, crossed through his bedroom and waggled his fingers, pulling magic from the world around to fluff out his bedding and set it aright, wicking away moisture from beneath the covers before it was fully covered. A small cantrip also warmed the entire bed, clearing out dust mites and other tiny miscreants. Toronto had a bad case of bedbugs, and while none were present here yet, it never hurt to take precautions.

While he eschewed magic most of the time, there were certain –things—like putting his bed –together—that he'd long learned to accept he would never get done without the convenience his gift provided. Such things were just a tiny bit too repetitive and futile for him to complete regularly, not after the first half century of trying.

Slipping outside to the hidden deck on the roof of his apartment building, he let the early morning chill fill his lungs. Heavy laden, moisture-filled air from the nearby lake surrounded him, causing him to shiver as he stood there in his pajamas, readying himself for his morning routine.

Gentle rotations and stretches, arms, wrists, hips, waist, ankles. Then, once he was sufficiently –limber—and it took longer each –decade—he began the slow and graceful qigong movements he practiced every day. Simple forms that looked like nothing more than hands waving around and hips twisting. It carried him a few feet, slippered feet sliding on damp flooring.

A last exhalation as he came to a stop, and he ran through a catalogue of which form to test next. He picked a baqua form for today; the circular nature of the technique reminding him of his own predicament, Mo Meng began.

Morning routines were important. Their familiarity grounded him, and the minor variations of each day allowed his mind to settle and find solutions to the predicaments that beset him. Each movement of the arm, twist of the hips, rotation of the ankles was another moment where his mind could churn over old problems, finding solutions.

Testing recipes and formulas alike, till he was done.

Exiting the building not long after, his breathing only a little heightened, Mo Meng turned away from the regular farmer's market and grocery stores he would visit to acquire the day's ingredients. While he could, and did, source some ingredients from his contacts across the world, the majority came from

Toronto itself. If he didn't need to keep his global connections alive, he might have sourced it all locally.

Well, within reason.

Modern commerce was amazing at providing foodstuffs from across the globe, but it had a tendency to do so by offering the same items, often picked slightly unripe to help with preservation. Even if he did have contacts for more esoteric or wider varieties, from apples to fungi, it never hurt to go to the source for products quick to ripen like bananas, or with more niche applications like durians.

Still, today was leftover day.

While he would need a few fresher additions, the majority of his ingredients would originate from the remainders in his kitchen, requiring significantly less time to prep. Or even less concern about the freshness or crispness of the ingredients.

After all, there were recipes and preparation methods to hide all that from all but the smallest number of customers.

It was one of the foibles of modern-day fine dining, where the emphasis was on the best –ingredients—wagyu meat, alba white Italian truffles, hop shoots, almas –caviar, that the skill of cooking with less than pristine ingredients, with less than stellar equipment, was forgotten, often disregarded.

Then again, maybe he was just an old man, raging at the clouds and the dusting of water as they passed by. Used to the way things were, unable or unwilling to change. Heavens and hells above and below, this century would challenge even an immortal fox.

So perhaps he was allowed a little obstinacy, a little rage. He knew he had a tendency toward that, as did all the old immortals.

Kensington market in Toronto was a strange set of streets, filled with odds-and-ends bohemian shops and family restaurants that clung on, desperately, against the pressures of gentrification. As he walked, he passed trendy restaurants, specialized food retailers, vintage and used clothing stores and handmade goods retailers. All of it, right next to old Chinatown, with its wide-open streets and streetcars and mix of old and new establishments.

Mo Meng wandered through the early morning crowd, mostly workers hurrying back and forth to work and cutting through the mostly empty streets. Occasionally he spotted other early workers, slipping out for a smoke or heading in to join prep for the lunch hour, and traded agreeable nods with them.

Occasionally Mo Meng would step up to a building, touching certain parts of the wall to leave hidden glyphs on message boards that only the magical could read. Job boards, all of them linked to one –another—but of course, there were a half-dozen such companies and he had to visit each board separately. Competing organizations, broken along national, cultural or financial lines.

Mostly, though, he was looking to trade words with his true targets. Early risers like him. Mother Vinodrogova who was already outside, watering her plants before it got too hot, the curbside flower beds still lush and green. Fønss, leaning against a balcony, a piece of wood and a whittling knife in hand. Over there, nearer where Chinatown proper started, Ba Tsiu, hawking *bao* from his roadside stall, ready to run the moment he spotted the police.

Friends, denizens of the magical and mundane alike. Each of whom had one much more important trait than their knowledge of the hidden world.

All of them gossips par excellence.

By the time he was done, Mo Meng was exhausted, mentally. Talking to so many, recalling the individual names, stations and ritual manners specific to each species or culture. There, a small gift of heartwood. Here, a seedling from a tropical plant. From Ba Tsui, at least it was –simpler—an exchange of money for a dozen buns that he gifted to those down on their luck, plus three he took for himself.

Finally, he was done.

Word would spread, and he had prep to begin.

After all, some of his dishes needed time to marry.

THREE
French Onion Soup

I t would not be perfect. Mo Meng had to remind himself of that fact, over and over again, as he dove into his work that morning. He was working with what he had, not what he wished he had. So the series of pans set before him, all set at medium heat and containing handfuls of onions, were a mixture of chopped and rough cut rather than all being the long tendrils that made for a better mouthful.

Multiple saucepans, onions thrown in and a couple of cups of water added to the sauteing onions. Rather than just the usual yellow Spanish onions, he had a few handfuls of shallots, red onions and white as well in the mixture, whatever had been previously prepped. Covers on the frying pans to allow it all to steam and cook, to release their juices and the sugar that was necessary for caramelization.

Much faster with the cover and steam method than to stand over the entire thing, waiting. He had a timer running, ten minutes just in case he forgot, though he would be back to check anyway.

Next up was the bread. Baguettes were the usual recommendation, day-old and dried out rather than fresh ones. He had few such loaves in the kitchen, but one of his tasks this morning had been to visit other bakers, taking their unsold bread off their hands. He had quite a variety, though he had enough to be picky with what he prepped for the French onion soup.

After all, day-old bread was useful for more than just soup.

So, long quick slices of the bread with the bread knife. Prep for later, because he would not be placing the slices in the soup just yet. That came at night, when the onions and the soup had cooked for a while and mingled properly, when the orders started coming in and he needed to warm it all up and melt the cheese just before serving.

Speaking of onions...

Mo Meng slipped back to his grill, where the smell of sauteing onions rose from the covered saucepans. He popped off the lids, lowered the heat from high to medium-high and began the process of stirring each of the pans. Caramelization would take a while, since the water would have to boil off and the onions take on a dark hue. Step away too early, get impatient and not let the onions darken properly, and the soup would not be as sweet as it could be.

In the meantime, it was time to add the various –spices—salt, pepper and a touch of sugar to speed up the caramelization process. He preferred cane sugar for this, to add another layer, though brown or white worked just as well. He'd taste it later, when he had a better idea of how the mishmash of onions he was using worked out, adjusting as he went along.

His eyes watered a little, the onions releasing their final revenge. He ignored it as best he could, though it didn't stop him from squinting and blinking repeatedly. Crying because of –onions—or the occasional forgotten finger in the eye after handling –chilis—was a rite of passage for a cook. Amateur or professional.

More importantly, the smell of the cooking onions pervaded the room, bringing a smile to his face. Stirring the onions one after the other, he moved to grab a couple of deep stock pots, many of them already filled with leftovers from the day before. Others had been gently boiling from the day before with leftover scrap meat and bones.

At home, if he had been cooking for himself or family or in a time when diners were less fastidious, he would have saved the bones from dishes eaten rather than just the discards. He would have boiled it all, extracting the nutrients and taste to create a proper bone broth. Muddied and swampy, requiring straining and often filled with layers of fat which he would skim off to save for cooking other dishes, but so full of flavor.

It –had—did—make his dishes unique, for each iteration would use a different combination of spices and meats. Subtle variations in depth and taste, requiring him to take extra care to even out flavor profiles, sometimes adding spice or peppers or salt. It had been a challenge he'd enjoyed, even if there were occasional failures.

Then again, you learned from your failures. Success only teaches you that you did it right, but a –failure—oh, it had so many lessons to offer. With each failure, a new series of lessons, new ways of doing something wrong. He treasured his failures almost more than his successes, because each failure was a scaffold for future accomplishment.

Pots on the boil, Mo Meng grabbed bundles of thyme and rosemary, tied them together and threw them in. He left the pots to return to the onions, stirring them further. Always stirring so that they did not burn, even as they slowly turned a rich, golden brown. All too easy, for a new chef, to stop, to get bored when it was just a little brown. That was always a mistake.

Deep and dark, all the sugars properly caramelized and yes, a little burnt. Patience required, like all good things, like the season's harvest or winning the trust of an injured companion.

Next up, wine. Red wine. Nothing too expensive, though he did have a few partially empty bottles waiting for use that were pricier. Not just red wine, though, because he was using up what he –had—and so he had some leftover rice wine and some white to add. The heavier liquors didn't really go bad, so he wasn't too worried about adding any of those from his stocks, though an open bottle of sherry waited to round out the flavors further.

He scraped the bottom of the saucepans after pouring the wine in, watching the mixture boil and soak into the onions. Mo Meng breathed deep, tasting the myriad scents, the deep impression of red wine and alcohol burning off, the dark onions.

Hands never stopping in their movements across the various pots, waiting as the wine reduced.

Eventually, the work was done, the liquid mostly reduced. He lifted the pans off the stove, one after the other, and deposited the contents into the boiling stock. Caramelized onion, dark and rich, and the alcoholic wine slurry, a swish of stock across the top of the pans to retrieve the last of the contents as it plopped into the pots, one after the other.

That done, he lowered the temperature, leaving the stock and onions to concentrate. With the pots uncovered, he just needed to reduce the soup further, tasting once in a while to make sure it was in-line with expectations and didn't need any additions. He had a few minor tricks up his sleeve, depending on the stock pot, to increase the depth of flavor if needed. Umami was the name of the game, though sugar might be required—but he had miso, mushrooms and, if all else failed, MSG granules.

However, for now, preparations for the starter of the day were complete and it was time to turn to the next dish. After all, he couldn't really have a tapas night with just one item on the menu.

FOUR
Extra Hands

Kelly winced as her phone vibrated inside her jacket again. The notification alert had been blinking consistently for the last fourteen hours, ever since she created the post for the restaurant as requested. She had turned off notifications during –class—and while –asleep—but in the few minutes when she checked, she'd seen the questions piling up.

Every time she answered, it had been like throwing chum to the sharks, causing a feeding frenzy of further enquiries. Even if her answers had been variations on 'It's a surprise!', 'Leftovers from the last few weeks' and 'I don't know'. She'd started posting that towards the end, when speculation about what was being made had grown too virulent.

Who would have thought that announcing you were going to dedicate a night to making leftovers could cause such rife speculation? Sure, every culture, every nation and race had their own variation of the leftovers meal. It made sense, after all. Food waste was something that only the very rich could afford—and often, not even that. Most times, the 'wasted' food was given to their servants to consume, or saved by their cooks to be repurposed later.

It was only modern conveniences and wastefulness that saw metric tons of food thrown away. For immortals or long-lived species, memories of eating scraped-together meals were still prevalent. Or so they were all too happy to tell her in long, artful messages. They might have learned how to text, but the advent of dictated messages had allowed their often verbose natures to come to the fore. Even Kelly had her own memories of such –times—like last night, when she'd grabbed a can of sardines and bread for dinner.

Slipping into the restaurant, she closed the door and scurried down to her usual seat after her usual entrance routine. She had arrived early enough to work the socials, quickly going through the various messages that needed answering before closing the laptop.

Once she was done with those extra duties, she began the process of readying the restaurant for the day. A broom took care of the dirt that had accumulated overnight, even as she eyed the lights high above to make sure none had burned out. As she worked, she glanced into the kitchen at times. Mo Meng had offered only the briefest of greetings before moving on, head bent over his various pots, pans and utensils.

Staring at the large number of utensils and napkins to be wrapped, she extracted earbuds from her pocket. A minor adjustment and her latest podcast on Appalachian myths—and the truth behind them as detailed by a southern vampiress—began to play. It amused her, a little, that an entire subset of the internet was cordoned off for the supernatural, accessible only to those who knew or cared to learn about the truth. A supernatural dark net, except less concerned with illegal behavior than detailing a history and culture that was blending all too quickly into the mainstream.

That she had been given the details of how to enter this hidden part of the internet had been acknowledgement of her shift in status, from ignorant mundane to slightly more knowledgeable mundane.

For now, that was more than sufficient.

Routine and a good podcast helped her get through the work, even if there was a lot of it. Scores of utensils to be wrapped, tables to be wiped down, glasses to be set aside and more water jugs filled. She was so busy and engrossed in her podcast and work that it required Mo Meng coming by to tap her on the shoulder to awaken her to the insistent knocking on the door.

"Guests?" he asked.

"Not that I know of..." Kelly sighed and straightened. "Let me talk to them." She hesitated, turned to him and added, "I will need the full menu, soon."

"Of course," Mo Meng said.

At the door, Kelly readied herself to deal with an annoyed customer—more often than not of advanced years—who'd arrived too early, certain in their belief they should be an exception to all rules of decorum and sense. She was thus surprised when she found a boy—a youth—barely taller than her own middling five-five. On the other hand, he had the most amazing green eyes, so deep and soulful that they made her want to stare.

Of course, right now, they expressed a worrying degree of impatience and concern.

"Is this Master Mo's restaurant?" the speaker asked, uncertainly.

"Yes," Kelly answered. "Who's asking?"

"Damian," the man answered. Short-cropped, curly red hair shifted as he peered inside, looked back and forth and then nodded. "I will speak with the Master now. Send for him and let him know I am here."

"I'm sorry, but we're closed right now. If you're a supplier, I can let him know. Otherwise, we're not taking solicitations or sales pitches."

"Sales pitches?" Damian straightened his back, his chin rising so he peered down over his nose. The effect was rather diminished by his height, though. "I am not here to sell things like a common merchant." He deflated a little. "I am here to be hired."

"Hired?" she repeated.

"As aid for the restaurant."

"Do you have any experience serving?"

"I have visited many, and partaken of delights all across the world."

"Uh huh." Doubt grew in her voice. "Have you actually worked in one?"

"No."

"I... well..." Kelly felt lost, thrown off by the sheer arrogance of the one before her. When Damian stepped closer, she backed off reflexively, allowing him to come all the way in. By the time she had turned, automatically closing the door, he was down the stairs and halfway across the floor, looking around in an almost proprietary way.

Proprietary and haughty, as though what he saw was not up to his standards. She bristled a little at that, only to see Mo Meng exiting the kitchen.

"Master Mo," Damian said with a formal bow. "I have been informed you seek aid in the running of your establishment."

"I do." Mo Meng's gaze raked over Damian. "I hold no prejudice toward your kind but..." Damian's eyes narrowed and Kelly gulped, a sudden frisson of fear shooting through her. The boy had gone from arrogant to something more, something dangerous. A cock of his head, a small smile, and as suddenly as it appeared, Damian's aggression faded. "...you have no experience working in a restaurant, do you?"

"No."

"I thought not." Mo Meng's lips pursed, gaze sweeping over the dress shoes, the designer clothing and expensive watch the other sported. "It will not be easy. And you will be tasked as befits your experience."

"I understand, Master Mo."

"Mo Meng. Or sir, if you have to. No master. I am taking no more students." Mo Meng continued to stare at Damian, then spun toward Kelly. She braced herself, catching that mischievous glint that had appeared in his eyes and realizing what was coming. "You said you needed help, yes?"

"I did, but..."

"Busboy."

She hesitated, having noted how Damian bristled and then settled after a moment.

"Can he do it?"

"We'll find out, won't we?" As though the matter was settled, he returned to his kitchen, leaving Kelly to stare at the other as he turned to regard her.

"Mistress." A slight bow, one that caused her to shake her head and send blonde ringlets swishing around her face.

"No, no, no. That'd give people all kinds of wrong impressions." She stuck her hand out. "Kelly. Nice to meet you."

He took it, shaking her hand firmly and quickly. Surprisingly warm hands, almost feverishly hot, but he looked fine. Almost excited, if she had to name the emotion. On the other hand, releasing it, she had to worry—that hand was all too smooth.

"And you." Damian hesitated, then stepped close, lowering his voice. "What, exactly, does a busboy do?"

She suppressed a sigh, knowing that everyone had to start somewhere. And really, how troublesome could it be, to show him what he had to do?

After all, she did need the help.

FIVE

Leftover Vegetables

Chaos and flame subtly beat upon the wings of magic, warming the air and altering the flow of energy in his restaurant. Mo Meng twitched his fingers, altering a few inscriptions and the flow of energy into them to deal with the new presence, noting how the entire arrangement strained. Even now, in the short time he had been here, the newcomer had begun to affect the building.

If Damian lasted, his ongoing presence would need to be accounted for. Minor alterations took care of the matter for today, but Mo Meng knew he would have to take further precautions in the future if the other became a fixture. Never mind the numerous other complications the boy brought with him.

A future problem, and one that might never arise. For now, it did little to change the matter at hand, or what his duties were at present.

From the refrigerator, he pulled a variety of leftover vegetables, products that verged on going from ripe to wilted. The ones that had tipped over too far, he set aside, cleaning and clearing them to be stored away, to be pickled or preserved. Some he sliced thin, others he kept whole.

Submersion of leftover vegetables in a liquid was a time-honored solution to excess. It did not matter what you pickled or preserved, in a way, because the solution itself and the appropriate amount of time would do the job. These days, of course, most people used glass jars, but Mo Meng had his own, age-old solutions. Large clay and porcelain jars with thick walls and cork seals, smooth stones taken from rivers and lava fields around the world.

He extracted the empty stone urns and began the process of filling them. He mixed and matched some mixtures, while keeping others like the cabbage, radishes and cucumbers by themselves so that they would not be contaminated when he used them in their familiar forms as side dishes or garnishes. When he had a few urns ready, he began to top them up. The type and variety of liquids depended on what he intended, what he felt like doing at the time. No specific recipes here, just a question of blending tastes.

White wine vinegar went into a twisting clay pot picked up four hundred years ago, from a potter in a village long destroyed. Stone urns, salvaged from a temple in the Songshan mountains, received ladles of rice or red wine vinegar. For others, he went with a brine solution – salt and water with additional spices or herbs in a spice bag to bring out different flavors. Dill, ginger, garlic, chilis, sugar and sesame oil were just some of the options here. He blended the techniques of various cultures and the taste profiles of various cuisines, stayed true to simpler recipes as he envisioned future meals.

Or, in some cases, decided to try something new.

That was the joy of cooking. Some might object to the idea that pickling itself might be called cooking, considering the lack of fire or heat or drama. After all, the process itself, the preservation of foodstuffs, was not considered part of the fine dining experience, the prestigious act of serving dishes to the wealthy. Rather, it was the work of the poor, the homemaker and the peasant.

Snootiness in the service of dollars, in other words.

Fast work, easy work, taking care of leftover vegetables. When he was done, he grabbed cheesecloth and stones and weighed the cloth down, so that the product was fully submerged. He checked on the first that he began, added a few more stones, and ensured nothing escaped around the edges. When he was satisfied, he sealed each one, using plastic sleeves with paper notes inside, listing contents, herbs and mixtures and dates, before he returned them to his storage room.

He felt the tug of magic as he opened the cupboard, noted the swirl of energy surrounding the door as he broke the seal. A slight twitch of his fingers as he manipulated the urns, shifting some aside. He placed his urn, sent it to the back, rotated the contents one by one. He checked the contents of those he pulled forward, eyeing the dates and extracting some for use later in the day with a flicker of power.

Funny how much more magic he was using. Not for the cooking, of course, but to help with the small things. Moving urns, cleaning on occasion, or verification of cleanliness. Opening portals to places to acquire ingredients or supplies, to check on recipes he might have forgotten the details of from the original chefs. It started with the necessity of the increased workload, but it also became a question.

Why he drew that line, so arbitrarily. Why he had grown so obstinate about magic use, to make extra work for himself when he didn't need it. Was he trying to prove himself? To whom? Was it that egoistical need to show that he didn't need magic, that it had no control over him?

It was a question that troubled him at times, as the pressures of a successful business pressed upon him. Wondering what he was sacrificing for his ego, whether he should swallow his pride again. He asked himself that question as he finished sorting out what he needed for later today, the door closing with a whisper.

The more customers he had, the simpler the recipes he had to make if he was to handle them all. Meals that were quick to cook, that required less focus and finicky preparation. It was why some dining establishments only had limited seats, a half-dozen, a dozen at most. Perhaps with more hands...

But that was for another day. Another time. Today, he chose to lean towards simplicity, finding bamboo skewers among his supplies and slipping the vegetables on, one after the other.

Was there a specific kind of technique, a magic needed for grilled vegetables over coals and wood chips? Not really. Oh, you could do things like adding special salts, infused oils or even painting with lard to create different tastes. There were details that mattered, of course, from the brushing to the soak to the wood, like the apple wood he had prepped, but even that would be at best a minor addition.

At the end of the day, roasted vegetables were simple but tasty. Salt, flames and fat, and just enough time to allow the sugars to caramelize. Control the heat and timing and you had a tasty meal, one served on long plates that could be done in batches and left to cool under a warming lamp.

Best of all, so long as he hadn't cut the vegetables too thin, it made perfect use of what he had left.

As for the rest of his vegetables, the ones that he'd diced and julienned and minced and more, well, he had plans for those too.

Six
Spring Rolls

There were a number of things one could use extra vegetables for. Of course, he'd fried and baked some leftover vegetables, simple recipes with a splash of soya sauce or sesame oil or a vinaigrette mixture that made the dish satisfying and tasty and easy to prepare.

On the other hand, you could also get a little more exotic with such leftovers. So long as the vegetables and herbs were fresh and you had sufficient vermicelli that needed to be used up, you could make spring rolls. Assuming, of course, you had spring roll skins lying around.

Considering that Mo Meng had a stack waiting to be used and on the verge of going bad, it was about time. Leaving them in the fridge covered in wax paper ensured that they did not dry out, but they only really lasted for a day or two before they went bad. Even magic could only help so much with such things, and he rarely utilized magic for storage purposes anymore. Not since the advent of refrigeration. No, spring roll skins, when you made them fresh, rather than relying on store-bought machine-made ones, only lasted so long.

Not to say there was anything wrong with those. After all, even professional chefs grew lazy, and many of the machine-made and mass-produced items did a good enough job. Not perfect, and sometimes—depending on the particular brand—the taste of preservatives and plastic was distinct. Still, they worked for when one was eating at home, cooking for oneself and in a rush, or when you were too exhausted after slaving over the stove to do anything more complex.

That was one of the secrets of most –chefs—what they ate, after days and nights of cooking food for others, was often significantly less glamorous than you would expect. Oh, there were –days—weeks even—when Mo Meng would test and retest recipes and take elaborate care with the type of meals he cooked for himself. More often when the restaurant had been quieter, the hours shorter.

But more often than not, these days, he had leftovers and simple meals, sometimes even takeout conjured from the surroundings.

A victim of his own success.

As for now, the large stack of spring roll wraps—made from rice flour and so thin that they were almost translucent—would make a lovely and simple appetizer. Rather than utilize prawns which he lacked, these spring rolls would be entirely vegetarian friendly, with a variety of fresh herbs—basil, mint, oregano the least among those he would add. Bean sprouts, rice vermicelli, scrambled –eggs—pre-fried and sliced into long thin –strips—as well as tofu slices—compressed by setting a weight on it and soaked for hours in soya sauce to add flavor—were among the main ingredients.

A variety of lighter vegetables and fruits added to the body, from julienned cucumber slices to carrots and purple or Chinese cabbage to fruits like mango slices—still firm—or peeled orange slices. In truth, anything that made enjoyable eating and that blended well together could be added to these fresh spring rolls, the only consideration the mouth-feel combination to give it the desired crunchiness and freshness.

Some items, of course, were to be avoided, especially for your average diner. Bitter melon was rarely appreciated; the same with okra or eggplant. Neither of the last two was traditionally eaten raw, and if overcooked had a tendency to sliminess. Peppers, on the other hand, both chilis and bell, could be added with an eye to the resulting mixture, the spice from the first a welcome addition, while the bell pepper could leave behind impressions of sad salads if overused.

Surprise ingredients in a dish could be a delight; a taste of sweet amidst a savory dish, a burst of umami-filled juice when biting into a bun. However, such experiences had to be controlled, carefully measured to ensure the surprise was pleasurable, a mouth-watering addition rather than an uncomfortable or lingering palate-tainter.

That was why Mo Meng went with more traditional flavor profiles, sweet or savory or slightly sour for each roll. A pair of dipping bowls, filled with peanut sauce and a mild rice vinegar, would allow the guest to further customize their eating experience. A little devilish part of him wanted to add barbecue sauce, but he refrained.

Traditional.

The process of rolling the spring rolls was routine. Place ingredients not in the center but near the side nearest to you. Allocate enough that it was a decent size, able to be squished a little but not too much. Apply a slight amount of water to fingers from a nearby bowl and then roll, using firm pressure on the ingredients and the wrapper itself, taking the edge closest to the body first and covering the ingredients before rolling it over once and then again. Once that was secured, you folded the sides before finishing the wrap, wetting the edge of the rice paper so that held together.

One, then another, fingers flying across the board, finished spring rolls appearing like magic to be added to plates. By the time he was done with the vermicelli, he had nearly fifty of them, with minor breaks in between to continue to stir various pots and pans, to check on the dishes on the grills and in ovens. A spell, muttered under his breath, kept the entire stack from drying out, so as to save the time needed to wrap everything in wax paper or plastic.

Fifty was a lot and not much at all, but a quick glance over at the pile of remaining wrappers made Mo Meng grimace. It was always deceptive, how many wrappers there –were—even after all these years. The thin layers meant that you were always underestimating how many were left, leaving you with either too little or way too much prepared ingredients.

However, he had found an easy solution to the problem a while ago. He might not have any more vermicelli, but fresh spring rolls were not the only dish that could be made with the wrappers. In addition, what he intended to do would cover many transgressions. In a quick flurry of movement, he extracted cold, ground meat from the fridge, pre-seasoned.

You didn't need to do much for the seasoning of the upcoming dish. Salt, pepper and, of course, five spice powder. Mo Meng made his own, since the venerable blend came in quite a variety of ratios and, frankly, quality. It was why you could purchase a half-dozen different off-the-rack spice blends and end up with differing tastes, even if the base should have been the same. Star anise, cloves, Sichuan peppercorns, fennel and –cinnamon—cassia cinnamon, not Ceylon.

Of course, if you wanted a little variety, there were other spices you could –add—Mo Meng's favorite being sand ginger powder, or shā jiāng fěn, which added a more aromatic and stronger taste than natural ginger. In this case, he dosed the meat liberally with the entire six-spice blend again and kneaded it in before washing his hands and returning.

Now the mixture was ready to be rolled into the rice wrappers. Adding various crispy vegetables and leaving out any of the softer additions like mango or orange ensured that the resulting spring roll would emerge from the deep frier with a good crunch, and not soggy.

Once more, prepping was a matter of routine. These spring rolls were half the size of the previous ones, the meat within only a millimeter-wide strip rather than stuffed to bursting. After all, these rolls were meant to be part of the tapas ensemble, not full meals by themselves.

Tonight, his customers would receive numerous small plates, all to use up the last of his ingredients. Which also meant using the last of the ground meat for another dish when he ran out of wrappers. Though what he planned for that, he wasn't sure.

Maybe fried rice. That was always a good fallback.

SEVEN
Opening Hour

Kelly kept an eye on the new help, curious how Damian would work out, how he would take orders. He worked hard, a burning intensity to each of his actions as she guided him through the basics of set-up before they opened. In some cases she had him repeat what she had done, just to get him used to the process.

Sweep the floors, place chairs back on the floor, wipe down tables and chairs to remove any lingering dust. Help put together cutlery and napkins for the upcoming dinner rush, fill jugs with distilled water and leave them in the chiller. Check that extra notepads and pens were available and that the old cash machine still worked, same with the debit card machine.

Familiarize him with the building, where things were behind the bar, the various drinks they –served—a smaller number now, especially as the alcoholic additions were few and far between. Wipe down glasses and rack them, cut lemons and limes and stack them for later use, fill the tub full of ice, review the dishwasher out and the various bins that were needed and finally, teach quickly how to use the industrial machines for cleaning, including the compost and garbage bins set aside for leftovers.

All that and more, even as she sought to finish her own work. Answer a few important last-minute questions, note down the menu as described by her boss, add a special mark on the number of desserts available. She could already envision the complexity of the evening, as dishes would run out long before some of the pickier customers would arrive.

Tonight was going to be a minor disaster. With limited quantities of numerous dishes, she would have to constantly update her list of items available. More than that, the idea of only serving –tapas—small plates meant to be shared by –diners—meant that she would be running back and forth, serving and clearing plates, just to ensure her diners had space.

Not as though Mo Meng went for overly large tables. Not that they had the space.

It was why, even if Damian might not be particularly practiced at taking orders or working in a restaurant, just having him act as a busboy, clearing plates and refilling water and perhaps even...

"How do you feel about taking names for the waitlist when it gets crowded?" Kelly asked. She knew it was not the best suggestion, something that a dedicated hostess might be required for, or an employee of longer standing. You needed a deft hand at managing some of the more belligerent customers, especially the foodies and food bloggers whose heads grew a little too large for their non-existent hats.

Sometimes, she really missed the quiet times of before.

Though her bank account was not complaining. That, and the occasional esoteric payment, made her smile. Flowers that had been planted in her apartment that never seemed to require watering, a string bracelet that denoted a favor owed by an older gentleman with slick hair and round eyes that twinkled with good humor, a seashell that she could put to her ear and hear the ocean, far away. Any ocean, anywhere in the world. And yes, they sounded different, especially to ocean-goers.

Weird and wonderful tips.

"Do we have a tablet and booking software, or are we still using pen and paper?" Damian intoned, then looked around pointedly till he spotted the clipboard. His eyes narrowed a little, before he continued. "Never mind."

"We don't really need anything more elaborate..." Kelly said, defensively.

"Of course, but some security would be good." Striding over to the clipboard, he glanced at the simple set of lines set aside for name, telephone number and party number before grunting. His fingers waggled over the top of it and to Kelly's surprise, old letters peeled off the board and floated in the air. Moments later, they drifted back down.

"What did you do?" she said, coming over to his side and peering down at the board.

"Showing you what your lack of safeguards might result in." He waved the clipboard around, making it harder for her to read, but after a moment she realised what he had done. A new space had formed between crossed-out names. "Another cantrip would allow the replication and insertion of names and numbers."

"Well, they'd never do that..." Kelly said defensively.

"How would you know?" Damian sneered.

She bristled at his words, even as he flipped papers till he reached the plain backing board. Holding the papers still, he began to wave his fingers again. Little runes and eldritch symbols began to appear, etching themselves into the wood as curls of smoke rose, bringing the smell of burning wood and a tinge of something rotten, like spoiled eggs. Her nose wrinkled, but within moments, the entire board was filled.

Letting out a satisfied grunt, Damian let the papers slip down and hung the clipboard back on its small peg. "And yes, I shall take over the duties of host and ensure it is carried out properly."

"You..." Kelly hissed, glaring at the dark-eyed man who turned an impassive mien on her, the slightest smirk on his lips. She forced herself to swallow the curses that threatened to escape in a most unladylike manner and stomped away as he began to fuss with the front area, finding the towels that were kept there in case of rain, the barf bags and old whiteboard menus. She was most of the way back to the bar before she turned around and shouted, "Just make sure you clear the dishes too, busboy!"

Satisfied at her vindictive pettiness, she returned to her own work. If he was so smart, he could figure the rest out himself.

Not doing her job properly. Really!

The regulars were the first to arrive: Jotun and Tobias, side-by-side and filling the small doorway, giant and dwarf respectively. They strode in, only pausing for a moment to jockey for the position of stepping in first, and stopped, briefly, to eye Damian. He had stepped over to try to slow their casual entry, only for Jotun to gently push him aside with one giant, meaty arm before the pair made their way to their regular tables. Jotun in the back, Tobias closer to the kitchen. Close enough that they could talk across the tables without shouting, but noisy during the busiest parts of the evening.

Kelly made a mental –note—again—to talk with them about shifting places on regular nights. Maybe even sitting together, perhaps. They did that half the time anyway, but it would save space and make it less rowdy when they eventually chose to argue over some arcane political matter or the latest hockey game.

Damian looked perturbed, unused to being ignored. However, it did not stop him from getting in front of the next in line, trying to create order from the sudden influx as the restaurant opened.

Kelly bit her lip, amused at his attempt to impose order on the initial chaos, and left him to it. Better for the boy to learn who the regulars were himself since he was so sure of himself.

Incompetent.

Hah!

"Good evening, Jotun!" Kelly chirped brightly as she came over with glass and pitcher. The big man was dressed in another plaid shirt, beard neatly trimmed, hunched over a little to hide his massive height. She poured the water swiftly, placing the pitcher on the table once she was done as per his preference. Same with Tobias, though Marilyn when she arrived would have been shocked at such service. "Did you read the menu we posted?"

"What menu?" Tobias rumbled from his seat, arms crossed over the barrel of his chest. He might be short, but he was nearly as wide as he was tall, with arms bigger around than Kelly's thighs. A reminder that she needed to hit the gym again every time she saw him. "'Assorted tapas and desserts served, tonight only!' isn't much of a menu at all."

"Well, it's what I was told. We have some roasted vegetables, French onion soup, a bread pudding for dessert, a stew and other assorted dishes. Do you want your usual order, then?" Kelly asked, eyes dancing with humor. "Perhaps just one serving this time, rather than two?"

Tobias grunted, "Anything to drink?"

"We have a few bottles of kefir, if you'd like one?" Kelly dropped her voice. "There's only a few remaining..."

"Done."

"Same. I shall follow the vertically challenged today," Jotun rumbled. "At least to begin."

"Who's vertically challenged, you—!"

Kelly coughed into her hands, gestured at the stream of newcomers. "Perhaps you could sit together, continue your conversation more quietly?" She waited a beat, while the pair looked hesitant, and added, "Please?"

"Of course."

"Sure."

That started a whole new argument about who was moving, but she knew they would work it out themselves. Best for her to leave them to it, or else they would try to drag her into the argument.

She slipped away, moving to drop the first orders off. She had barely needed to write anything for Tobias; so regular was the older man's order that she had prepped it already. Jotun's required adjustment, but she put the two together and moved on, taking more drinks and water from behind the bar to serve the newcomers as the restaurant filled.

No slow start for today.

EIGHT

By the Prickling of my Thumbs

Mo Meng tilted his head to the side as he worked, parboiled potatoes draining and drying in a colander over the sink as he moved on to the next task. Damian had slipped into the kitchen, pulling open the refrigerator nearest to the entrance and peering within, frowning.

"Looking for something?" Mo Meng asked curiously, as he added spoonfuls of baking soda to the pot of boiling water, carefully dropping wedges and other smaller potatoes and potato slices into it.

He set a timer once he was done, closed the lid on the baking soda container and put it away.

"Kefir," Damian said. "I'm supposed to bring the bottles we have to a guest."

"Outside, under the bar in the minibar refrigerator," Mo Meng corrected the other easily. "There's eleven bottles ready."

Damian shut the door, nodded and strode right out. No word of thanks, barely even acknowledging the instructions. Mo Meng snorted, even as he turned his attention back to his potatoes. These would be the major source of carbohydrates, and while the grill was warming up and the roasted vegetables he would grill would add to the taste, these would be a highlight.

On that note, he needed to ensure that the garlic butter sauce was ready. Opening a small ramekin, he fished out the pre-baked garlic, the cloves already separated from the paper shell, baked in the oven with real olive oil and softened by the heat so its sweetness would be more pronounced. He smashed them flat in the ramekin, mashing them together before he dropped the contents into a waiting pot of melted butter.

Freshly roasted garlic and butter smells drifted up as he mixed the two together, a smile growing on his lips as he threw in a touch of salt. There was a second batch of basting sauce that would skip the garlic seasoning, for those customers who were a touch more sensitive to the purifying effects of the herb, but this, this was his preference.

Moving on, he stood over the stove, leaning over to peer at the boiling sauce. Bright red from sweet paprika and tomato sauce, it had been made by combining broth and vinegar with a dash of cornstarch to thicken the dish. Normally, the recipe called for a vegetable broth so as not to dilute the taste of the paprika, but in this case, Mo Meng had used a combination of what he had on hand. It would muddy the taste a little, marring the perfection of the dish.

A little difference, to make the final recipe a little more interesting. He did, however, stir the sauce to make sure it wasn't clumping together, take a spoonful to taste, and add a touch more salt. He kept stirring, for this was a thick, drizzly sauce, not a clumpy or runny one. It would be ladled onto potatoes later, or perhaps set aside in a dipping bowl.

Feet carried him onwards once he was content, never stopping. There were too many things to do, not enough time to do it. From the oven, a baking tray was extracted, greased down so that the dried potatoes he took from the colander would not stick. He used the back of a glass to help smash the potatoes flat so that they'd be about a quarter of an inch thick. Not too thin, or else the potatoes would burn. Not too thick, or else they would not crisp. The pot of warm garlic butter was used on the top, generous dabs all across before adding more salt and pepper and a generous handful of chopped rosemary across it all.

Back into the oven, another tray pulled out as he continued the process. On and on, moving from boiling pot to grill to stove, checking on his various dishes till it was time to pull the first tray out.

Once extracted, he flipped the potatoes quickly with a spatula, noting how they were beginning to dry and crisp. Another generous application of butter—always more butter and fat, that was the way to heart attacks and good taste—before it went back into the oven. Repeat with every other tray within.

Switching between ovens helped him keep track of what was where, and allowed him to check on the contents of the other dishes he had cooking, a verification that he hadn't burned the cheese or spoiled the meat.

A quick eyeball verified their doneness before he moved on, the tray with newly readied potatoes held in hand, towel draped over the edges as he scooped the pieces onto waiting plates. A half-dozen of the baby potatoes or wedges per plate, smashed flat with crispy edges showing. Four plates, all done in moments before he set the tray down.

Of course, he had to finish the dish first. That required more than just a sprinkling of sea salt and fresh chives, but also the sauce. For that, he spooned brava sauce into tiny serving ramekins, a nod to the Spanish origins of the evening. He could have added a garlic mayo aioli sauce to this, taking it from bright red to a pale yellow; but there was enough garlic on the plate as it stood.

Fresh paprika in the sauce and garlic baked potatoes releasing their distinctive scents, mingling together as he dropped the dishes on the pass. He called out to Kelly that service was ready before he went to prep the next batch.

Simple dishes today, just a lot of them.

It was as he was turning away to move back to his grill that he felt it. An itching in his thumbs, a twisting in the air, a shape forming in the boiling pot of water. Hooded and dressed in a robe to cover face and body against the non-existent chill of summer. Head lowered, long hair escaping the cowl, old-fashioned dress nearing her ankles.

He shivered at the sight. Just as quickly, it disappeared, the prophetic image breaking apart in the soup. It could have just been coincidence, if one was wont to believe in that. A fluctuation in the ether, a twisting of the threads. A warning of the one that was coming.

And what that boded, he knew not.

Not yet.

Nine

Orange and Assorted Fruit Kefir

The requirements to make kefir were simple. A sugar—potentially contained in the liquid itself—a liquid and the kefir grains. You could make it in a variety of vessels, though optimal temperatures and environment would speed up the process. A simple fermented drink, and the kefir grains could be reused to continue the process in other vessels as needed. Milk and water kefir were the most common fermentation types, though modern times had seen experimentation and the production of a variety of different liquid-based kefir drinks.

In this case, Damian was carrying a water-based kefir, one that utilized the sugars of the various fruits and orange juice that had been introduced to allow the drink to ferment. It was probably one of the easiest drinks to make at home, though the exact process always required a touch of management.

The entire process just took time, and produced the bubbles that gave the drink its fizzy, very mild alcoholic content, along with a high amount of pro-biotic remnants.

Damian set the first bottle down beside Tobias, and paused to open the flip-top cap. It released with a satisfying pop that brought a small smile to both their grim faces. It was wiped away quickly, neither wishing to spoil their good reputation with an excessive degree of joy.

At least, in Tobias's case, not until he ate and drank. After all, the proper appreciation of food and drink was one of the few widespread and emotional expressions of joy and contentment that a dwarf was allowed. Even in the process of refining ore and the melding of iron, a dwarf never expected to showcase deep and heartfelt satisfaction. It would encourage the Deep Dwellers to rise and insult the Lords of the Forge, to embrace joy over such minor successes.

No, food and drink and special occasions were the only time one could wholeheartedly express satisfaction. The first and second because they were transitory, unlike their real works. The last, because what kind of dwarf would they be, to not celebrate births or grieve the death of loved ones?

Tobias blinked, realizing his attention had drifted. The newcomer was gone, leaving a filled glass of kefir, glinting gold and pink with bubbles edging the drink and rising to the surface to disperse in the air.

He raised the glass to his nose, breathing deep. Oranges, of course, hints of raspberry and strawberries which likely provided the additional color. Grapefruit too, he could see in the bottle along with a handful of raisins. The drink smelled fruity, not even a trace of alcohol to be found. He was reminded of fruit juices from his past, a rare enough treat in olden times when his clan had faced more trying circumstances.

Fresh fruit laid out for the picking any time of the year was a rarity, a delicacy that only the sun dwellers and the rich might have. Instead, his people made do with fermented and pickled fruits and *klak*. And only masochists liked eating *klak*.

Hesitation over, he let the cool glass touch his lips, brush his beard. Felt the bubbles gently prick at his tongue as he tipped the drink back, felt the cold liquid wash down his throat. Not too bubbly, so that he felt the need to burp. Sweet and clean, with just the hint of a bite. Complex fruity flavors that brought with them memories of summer.

All of it washing into his mouth, down his throat. Before he knew it, his glass was empty, his eyes sparkling, and a hand was reaching for the bottle. Only for Tobias to sternly caution himself to take care. Joy was clear, was allowed, but greed and haste—never.

Still, he did take another sip once he had poured himself another cup.

Arms crossed before him, Tobias settled in to wait for what else would be brought forth.

TEN

It's Getting Warm in Here

Inside the kitchen, Mo Meng was working quickly now that orders were arriving. He had to chuckle at the first two, which read 'all of it', with more selective orders arriving afterwards. Still, it did mean that he had to get the soups in the oven, throwing cheese, bread and then more cheese into the ramekins before slipping them onto a tray for heating. The half-dozen bowls were placed in the oven before he moved on, a mental note made of when to return to grab the melted cheese dish.

Next, he checked on the pair of steamers. Industrial sized steamers, each of them four and a half feet across, they sat rather low to the ground with a massive, bubbling pot beneath. Multiple stacks of large bamboo steamers—more often used to steam buns—were laid across them, awaiting their contents.

Those, Mo Meng was just about finished prepping. Glass bowls filled with marinated leftover pork, premixed with the traditional black bean sauce, and then a small scattering of additional, whole beans added for visual effect, if not taste. The leftover pork had come from pork shoulders, rib ends, loins and other trimmings over the past few days, a mixture of lean and fatty pieces. A preference for fattier cuts for this dish; but it could be made with any cut, as he was showing.

The marinade itself was a simple recipe, bolstered by the addition of Shaoxing rice wine, ginger, garlic, sugar and salt to the fermented black beans and a generous helping of cornstarch to provide a coating over the ribs and reduce the effect of the hot steam. Marinaded for an hour, the dish was then placed with some oil into the waiting bowls before they were added to the steamers.

Ten minutes and the dish would be finished. Mo Meng kept readying bowls, knowing that once the orders started flowing, he would have little enough time to get on this. There was nothing wrong with steaming the dishes a little longer, the only major effect being to make the meat softer and less springy.

Not your typical tapas dish, unless one considered dim sum a tapas event. It did follow the same ideology, after –all—small dishes, generally moderately priced, ordered in the half-dozens for sharing with a group as a social event. If not for the differing –times—brunch and dinner—when they were traditionally served, they might have been the same thing. In concept at least, if not execution.

Strange, how such things crept up and repeated in humanity's past.

Maybe it would be the same in the future, though concurrent ideas and inventions were all too common now, perhaps because of the interconnection of the world. Images beamed from one pole to the next, so that ideas and vision intermingled, forming unusual inventions and circumstances their progenitors might never expect.

Like a tapas dish mixed with dim sum.

Who knew what the future might bring?

Well, probably his latest guest. After all, it was one of her many gifts.

Unusually for him these days, he debated exiting the kitchen. He could, with a touch of magic, ensure that nothing burned. If he really wanted to, there were spells that could slow down time in the kitchen, buy him some time for conversation.

For this guest, it might be politic to do so. After all, she could be touchy at times, and he certainly wouldn't want to be cursed out for poor manners. At the same time, he had heard she'd mellowed a little, ever since the 1960s.

A moment's debate, and he reached sideways, pulling forth a sliver of his power. He wove it together and sent it along, a greeting invisible to any but those with the right sight. It would have to do.

After all, just because he could didn't mean he should. That was perhaps the first unspoken rule of magic. The amount of work he had to do was never-ending. The problem with promising a dozen dishes was that one had to actually cook them.

ELEVEN

French Onion Soup (2)

"No, I'm sorry. We really don't have any public electrical outlets. You'll have to make do with your battery."

"But it's not working! I swear, I charged it before I left."

Kelly offered a conciliatory smile to the young lad looking down at his assorted electronics in frustration. She understood it, but could not help him with his problem. If not for the fact that he was willing to take the smallest and meanest table, she would have refused service to him and his electronics. Instead she left him alone as she spotted another guest arriving. Something told her that this was not a customer to be left waiting.

An older woman, slightly bent over and short. Extremely –short—barely topping five feet with her hunch. She might have been pretty once, when she was younger, but could only be described as striking now. Skin wrinkled and slightly dried, minor liver spots on face and hands. Dressed in a voluminous peasant skirt in brown and grey and an old army coat, patched multiple times, with numerous pockets filled to the brim. Kelly spotted dried herbs, string and a couple of pill bottles poking out of them.

"Party of one?" Kelly asked as she reached the newcomer. A nod confirmed her guess, and she looked inside, finding a couple of tables left. No complicated seating charts required here. She led the lady over, pulling out a chair for her as she arrived at the table, set just a little off the main kitchen window and near the bar exit. Good location, but a little noisier than some others, though it did put her within a few tables of both Tobias and Jotun.

Kelly noted the lack of reaction by either party, no indication of concern or recognition as the woman took her seat. Strange, for intuition told her that this was no normal guest. Much like the pair themselves, or Marilyn, or some of the other guests who came in less frequently; the herb lady was special. She was sure of it.

"I'm Kelly. I'll be your server today. Can I start you off with some water?"

"Water will do. Clear and fresh as a spring." Grey eyes lifted, regarding Kelly. "Are you of the old stock then, from the fair isles, Ó Ceallaigh?"

Kelly shook her head. "Maybe. My family just liked the name..."

"You should find out. It is always good, to know one's roots." Dark eyes caught Kelly's, and something moved in the older woman's gaze, a suction drawing the waitress into them. "Look into the past, for the future grows tumultuous. A locus forms, a blaze has been set. Dig deep, for the future burns."

Something built behind those eyes, something ominous. Kelly began to shiver, goosebumps and chills racing up her body. Intuition told her to turn away, but curiosity kept her gaze locked on the other. There was more to be learned, more to know, and all she had to do was look. Look into eyes that were dark and ancient, that held the weight of years gone by and whose depths contained hints of the—

A plate, dropped onto a metal counter, shattered the moment. The noise echoed through the room, louder than it should have, reverberating through the restaurant. It drew all their attention, breaking Kelly out of her trance. At the pass, Mo Meng stood, ramekins and plates arrayed before him like troops about to enter battle.

"Professor Southeil. Kelly is quite fascinating, but she has tasks to carry out. Perhaps another time, for your tidbits of wisdom, yes?" Mo Meng kept his voice low, a smile in his voice—but his eyes, his eyes were serious. None of the usual good humor present. "Another place, not here."

The regulars, the unusual members of the restaurant, were now paying attention, looking at the unassuming older woman and the owner. A few tensed, Jotun frowning, while Tobias had set his utensils down before him. The normal patrons looked a little amused, the few that could be bothered to look up from their phones.

"You never did like them, did you, Master Mo?" Leaning backwards in her chair, lacing fingers between each other, she continued. "Professor, Doctor, they both work. I'm working now and only teaching in the evenings."

"Healing or...?"

"Biochemistry."

Mo Meng inclined his head, and then shifted his attention to Kelly. With a start, she realized she was still standing beside Southeil, and with a bob of her knees, stepped away. She moved fast, shaking off the lingering ominous feelings. You had to get used to the strange and different in this job, and there were still dishes to deliver, water glasses to be filled and orders to be taken.

Just as quickly, thoughts of what had been faded into the background of her mind.

The words disappeared from her thoughts as they echoed and burrowed within, finding space in her subconscious.

Spoon engulfed in his large hands, tapping against the crust formed from melted shredded cheese, small portions of it falling over the edge of the white ramekin. A slightly stronger impact broke the crust, allowing melted cheese to ooze upwards and the broken edges of old, soaked bread to turn. The smell of caramelized onions and stock drifted from the ramekin, sweet and rich at the same time.

French onion soup on a cold day. What else could a giant ask for?

Gently pushing down on the bread, watching the liquid slip into the metal spoon, little flakes of onion floating in the dark soup. He raised the spoon, sipped, ignoring the slight burn as the hot liquid slipped into his mouth.

Sweet.

Savory.

An explosion of subtler flavors. A touch of garlic, a heavier bite from the sherry. Heat from the pepper, and maybe some chili? The stock was rich; darker and more flavorful than usual, a trace of beef perhaps. The onions had no texture, cooked down so much that they came apart at the slightest pressure. Translucent and plentiful, stringy and long.

He swallowed the mouthful and smiled hungrily.

The spoon dipped again, even as the smell of the soup rose up once more, tickling at his senses. Cheese and bread bits, a sprinkling of green on top to give color to the various shades of yellow cheese. White, pale yellow, dark and black where portions had burnt. Gouda, parmesan, Swiss, something else? Hard to say, there were so many.

He broke off a piece of bread and cheese, made sure to dunk it deep to soak it thoroughly, and raised the concoction to his lips. Drank deep, chewing on the soaked bread, still with a tiny bit of crunch after being dunked and warmed, the bread itself toasted beforehand.

The cheese was sharp, a touch bitter and gooey. He chewed on the bread and cheese together, working the mouthful between his teeth as trickles of captured soup escaped. He swallowed, feeling the warmth of the soup enter his body, bringing with it memories of heavy soups and cold winters. Warm liquid, sharp cheese, bread.

A familiar meal, though in larger quantities, sometimes even enough for dinner. Voices of his clan all around, some lost to time and the reaper's scythe, others to the passage of boats and bad decisions. All of them seated in a massive stone building, a clan hall filled to bursting and illuminated by flickering torches.

A long time ago, a simpler time.

Not better, though. Too many of his people had a tendency to look backwards, lament how things had been better—when life was simpler, the decisions that had to be made more limited. In doing so, they ignored the hard times; when famines swept the land because of a bad growing season, when battles over a cow or piece of land or a stolen woman would sweep aside a fragile peace. Blood and death and the stink of unwashed bodies, the times when they had to leave behind friends and family to be eaten by vermin rather than as a gift to the sky.

It was his curse, his burden, to have the clearest memories of his people. The ability to recall events as though it was yesterday, picture perfect. A magic of their people, given to their Clan Head. Memory to offer context, to provide –wisdom—or at least that was the theory. It was not always so, of course. Memory was only knowledge, and as humanity had learned from the Internet, one could still be ignorant with all the knowledge of the world at one's fingertips.

Wisdom was a choice, and a painful one at that.

Still, it was his duty to draw his people forth into this new future. Knowing what they had left behind, treasuring the parts of their heritage that mattered while forging new traditions for the future. Even if so many refused to believe him or his words, even as they struggled against his leadership and the things he demanded of them.

Spoon scraped ceramic, and Jotun blinked. Empty. He had consumed it all, and only a light coating was left, a lingering taste and memory of the soup. He frowned, scraping at the sides of the dish, pulling away melted cheese from the rim as he considered another order. Knowing that there were limited quantities today, and hesitation might mean regret.

Then again, all of Mo Meng's dishes were like that. A delightful concoction, that tantalized the senses and demanded a second helping.

So perhaps, wait and try it all.

After all, even a giant could only eat so much.

Decisions, decisions, decisions.

TWELVE
Stir the Pot, Full of Trouble

Mo Meng wandered over to the large pot, the one filled with scraps of beef and lamb. If you were making a meal of leftovers, there was clearly one dish that had to be made.

Stew.

Now, there were numerous kinds of stew in the world. Mediterranean, Irish, Dominican, Persian, Korean. It could be said that any culture had a stew variation, depending on how you framed the definition. After all, the basics of such dishes were simple. Brown the meat, add stock—or water—and vegetables and slow cook for hours, allowing the heat and salt to combine and break down the ingredients.

Depending on the source and location, you'd add more or less salt, more or less vinegar, or an alcohol to help break down the meat. Chilis did the same in some cultures, the chemicals in the spice helping to make even the toughest piece tender.

While Mo Meng would never consider himself knowledgeable about every recipe in the world, he had sampled and tested quite a few in his centuries. Admittedly, some of the more recent inventions—cuisines created in the last century through need and necessity—were not to his taste. Korean army stew and Hawaiian Spam cuisines were the kind of thing that he did not much enjoy, though he admired the versatility and creativity of the original chefs.

All that said, he had chosen to go with a more western approach this time. In this case, red wine added to the bottom of the pot after browning the meat, reducing it and then adding large amounts of vegetables and stock before slow cooking the entire thing. He had thrown in various spices as he saw fit, some dried shiitake mushrooms to give it further body, small amounts of chili and cumin. Juniper berries and allspice and herbs. No potatoes, since he had another use for them, but he did have some leftover barley.

Stew—add what you had, especially the off-cuts, the cheap pieces of meat, the slices that were tougher and chewier than the finer cuts. Fattier or tendon-filled pieces were the best, since they helped break it down better. Head bent over the pot, he raised the spoon he had used to stir it, eyeing the consistency. He tasted it and reached over to add another cup of stock rather than let the stock burn.

He breathed in the aroma, the variety of spices and the depth of flavor from the stock he had used. Mixed stock, chicken and beef and pork bone and meat, leftovers from his cuttings and trimming. Baked first before being boiled, to darken and amplify the flavors. The smell of the mushrooms, the light simmer of barley, the heaviness of the beef and lightness of the pork.

A small smile, as he brought another small spoonful into his mouth, tasted the dish. He added a touch more salt, not too much since he'd just diluted it with stock. Better to wait, taste again in a bit. The stew was ready; he just needed the newly-added stock to warm a little more before it was ready to be served.

In the meantime, he had other meals to prepare, more French onion soup to pull out. The potatoes were ready, so plated those and set them on plates for serving next. He dropped them off at the pass, paused long enough to glance at the tickets and nod to Damian as he came by, carrying dirty dishes.

For all his inexperience, the boy was moving with ease, stacking multiple dirty plates together and carrying a pair of empty water flasks. His head kept turning, side to side, listening to the thrum of conversation as he moved, his designer shirt at odds with the more casual clothing of the patrons.

Mo Meng started to turn, stopped as he spotted the latest addition to his restaurant. The old woman—Ursula—had a guest, a tea set before her and a cup of tea in her hands.

"Oh, that's not going to end well," he muttered.

Thirteen

Parboiled, Smashed Garlic Baked Potatoes

Ursula smiled, wrinkles deepening as she pushed the cup of tea towards Marilyn. "Drink. Drink well and fully."

Marilyn smiled, the natural tan of her Mediterranean heritage set off by ruby red lips turning up as she did as she was asked, draining the black tea in one swift motion. She set the teacup down, only for Ursula to take it and turn it clockwise three times. She tapped the teacup on the table once and then tilted it gently, humming a little as she stared into it.

"It's good that Mo Meng still uses loose leaves to brew tea in the old way. None of these fancy metal strainers or strange contraptions. Makes a mess of the foretelling, I tell you," Ursula said. "How are you supposed to read the turning of fate and destiny when it's all mixed up with the dregs of everyone else's fate, I ask you?"

"I truly do not know either," Marilyn replied. "On the other hand, they do brew better tea that way. Less leaves to pick out, and when it's put in a proper aeration device…"

"Not all of us are that picky," Ursula replied. Then, after a moment, she relented. "They do make better tea, and I do like how it purifies and distills the taste. Sometimes, though, I feel it lacks … variety. As though our desperate search for purity makes us forget that some of the best things come from the mixture of unexpected events. Why, you only need to see how we got penicillin."

Marilyn nodded in agreement, though her gaze tracked to the cup. Ursula snorted, tapping the cup hard with one long fingernail.

"Nothing in there for you to be concerned with. A meeting with an old friend, a gathering you'll want to miss, and a long lost item to keep an eye out for."

"A lost item?"

"I see bright colors, a memento. Most likely a photograph or painting," Ursula said. "You didn't pose for anything, did you?"

"A few. I did enjoy the Renaissance..." The dark-haired beauty's gaze grew lost and thoughtful.

"Well, best start watching, then."

"Of course, Mot... m'lady."

"Don't m'lady me. I'm a working woman, always have been." She waggled a finger in front of Marilyn, the dark-haired woman smiling wider at the chastisement. "Not like some of you."

"Good investments can see one through much. So long as it is broad and wide," Marilyn said. "Speaking of..."

"Bah! Ask Nostra for that, don't talk to me. I don't dabble in that side of things," Ursula grumbled.

"Not even a hint?"

Before the argument could devolve, Kelly stepped in, dropping a plate of delightful-smelling potatoes on the table. Her gaze sliding between the two women, she asked, "Should I set a second place here, then?"

"Eat with this old harlot?" Ursula eyed Marilyn who returned the look calmly. "Oh, very well. At least she has the good manners to greet me. Unlike some others!"

"I'm busy!" Mo Meng's voice trailed out from his kitchen where he was bent over, hands working furiously as he flipped over skewers of roast vegetables, never missing a beat. Somehow, even over the drone of industrial sized fans and the chatter of the other customers, he heard her.

"Very good." Kelly dutifully ignored the byplay. Like any good waitress, she was unobtrusive and efficient when necessary, chatty when it was quieter. A perfect complement to the diners' experience, and right now, necessarily silent. In seconds, she was back with the second plate and utensils for Marilyn, though Ursula was not waiting.

Spearing the still piping hot potatoes, she leveled the silver-dollar-sized coin-shaped delicacy to her eye level. As she did, the smell of roasted –spuds—baked until a firm and crispy outer layer was formed, melted butter and garlic slathered on it—wafted upwards, the sight of large sea salt crystals and fresh basil intermingling in the air and causing her mouth to water.

"Good. I'd be worried if there were no potatoes," Ursula said. "Such a great addition. Much better than turnips," her spotted nose wrinkling a little at the last word.

"Oh, hush. I like turnips. And radishes. And carrots," Marilyn said, picking up the potatoes. "Bread, too. Always a pleasure, fresh baked bread."

"You would," Ursula sneered, before taking a bite. There was an audible crunch as she bit into the potato, the smashed potato's crusty outer coating breaking beneath her teeth. Eyes widened a little at the audible crunch, the crack of hardened potatoes, the garlic and butter intermingling in her mouth as salt crystals intermingled with her saliva.

Simple flavor combinations with different surfaces. After the initial hardened crust, though, the inside was soft and chewy like a baked potato, a surprising textural difference. Not too much, of course, not when the entire thing had been crushed down to a quarter inch height.

Interesting to see how Mo Meng had varied the size, using his leftovers. Some of the potatoes were crispy all the way through, the butter and oil glaze making it taste like a thick crisp. Others were thicker and fatter, leaving a chewier center in the middle.

A variety of textures and tastes, and when shared between the pair, a point of contention as they fought for their favorites. Not that there was much overlap. Ursula for the thinner, crisper ones, Marilyn for the thicker.

As Ursula chewed and swallowed her potato piece, a piece done all too soon, further remnants of the dish were disappearing down Marilyn's throat. Eyes narrowed, Ursula sped up, discontent at being robbed of her meal showing in her every movement.

"I thought your kind didn't like garlic..." Ursula asked, out of the corner of her mouth.

"Only the young ones have real trouble. For the rest of us, it's just a minor discomfort. Heartburn, if you will."

"Well then, stop. No reason to hurt yourself!"

"I will once you stop slathering your pieces with butter. It's no good for your heart, especially one so ancient."

"I'll show you ancient!"

For a time, silence descended over their table as they quietly contested for the first and then the second plate of garlic smashed potatoes. Only when the next dish of roasted vegetables, one filled with a portion of red and green peppers, mushrooms, eggplant and turnips arrived did the pair slow.

"Yours," Ursula said, pushing the plate and skewer over.

"No, yours." Marilyn sniffed. "I prefer meat."

"Then you shouldn't have been eating my potatoes!"

"I can make exceptions."

"Then make an exception now. Eggplant." A theatrical shudder. "The Lord really was having his fun, when he made that one."

"What makes you think it was him, and not one of the angels? Fallen, of course."

"Good point," Ursula said. She rubbed her chin. "We could ask..."

Kelly, hearing their conversation, drifted over long enough to add. "No summoning demons in the restaurant, please."

"What? You already have one working here," Ursula said, glancing over at the quiet and arrogant boy strutting by, head held high and plates stacked in his hand. As though the dirt and mess from the plates could not touch him. The fact that his white shirt was still spotless was proving it true.

"We do...?" Kelly trailed off, looked at Damian. Her normal professional waitress smile slipped for a moment. Ursula stared, curious to see her reaction, only to be surprised as she rallied after a glance towards Mo Meng. Then again, the man always had the best of luck finding good help. "More water, ladies?"

"Kefir," Marilyn said. "And do not worry. He isn't the real thing anyway. Not really."

"Oh, I see." Kelly didn't, of course, but Ursula was not going to be the one to enlighten the sweet child.

Letting the mundanes in, that had to be done one step at a time—lest they run away, screaming and hunting for the nearest witch finder. And they all knew how that ended.

FOURTEEN
Making Do with Others

Ignoring the commotion outside, intent on clearing up the last of his acquisitions from the various bakeries he had visited, Mo Meng opened the fridge and extracted the pre-cooked flatbreads, the additional roti the bakery down the street had made.

He could have made the flatbread himself, or at least bought the dough and then flipped it, but not only did he not have the space—or time—to prepare the dish, that was not the point of the evening. Sure, the chilled pieces of bread were no longer as crisp and fresh as before, having been left in the fridge—covered or not—for hours. Not even warming it up would make it as fresh.

If he wanted to make a perfect dish, Mo Meng would have started from scratch. The point of today was to give himself a little break, to take a few shortcuts and make use of whatever was available. In this case, premade roti parathas from a trusted bakery, that would blend well with the rest of his ingredient leftovers.

Anyway, he only had two dozen of them here. Might as well do something fun with the remainder rather than worry about perfection. That was the advantage of cooking, that even failures were quick to disappear.

Beaten eggs, their yolks dark yellow and lovely, were the first ingredient. Salt, pepper, a dash of paprika for color and taste, cumin and cinnamon to add to the spices being blended. He debated adding something more, like turmeric or even chili powder. A small kick and color change, but he chose to go with this for now as he continued beating the mixture with one hand, waiting for it all to blend in before turning to the waiting frying pans.

First, though, he checked on the rest of his dishes, pulling out trays of soup or flipping meats before returning, bubbles from the egg mixture popped, the liquid settled. Fingers passed over the top of the heating pans, waggling back and forth above them as he tested the heat levels.

Perfect.

A quick dash of ghee into the pan; the reduced and clarified butter meant a higher cooking point while adding a more intense taste to the dish. He spread it around, made sure it was warmed before he poured a generous dollop of the egg mixture in. Immediately, the pan sizzled, the smell of cooking egg and butter rising up.

Before it could cook through, right on top the thin layer of swirled omelet, he dropped the roti. He let the egg and bread rest for a moment, just long enough for the pair to meld together, for the bread to warm a touch before he flipped the combination over.

Warm bread smells rose, crisping under the flame and heat. He lowered the temperature a touch, not wanting to scorch the bread, just warm it. Along the edges of the roti, egg mixture danced as it crisped, escaping from the bready underlayer.

The spatula moved, shifting the bread around so that it would not stick, testing movement and watching the dish like a hawk. Too long and it would burn, the egg would dry out entirely. If he kept it moving, controlled the temperature right, the last of the egg mixture would finish cooking. Then he raised one side, rolling it into a crispy cylinder to be set aside on the cutting board.

He waited for it to cool a little, repeating the actions on the next egg and roti combination, taking his hands off the pan and spatula long enough to portion the cooled mixture and place them on a plate before returning to his dish.

Getting ready to deliver it all to the front.

Sometimes, the simplest things in life were the best.

"Now, remember—we have to keep the receipts, and our stipend is heavily restricted." Mika was lecturing O, his companion and partner, as they stood outside the restaurant in the cold, waiting their turn to enter and add their names to the list.

"I know, I know. I don't know why we still have to follow the rules when they're obviously not..." Ophelia grumbled, hunching in a little under her well-cut dark blue pantsuit. The clothing was more appropriate for a high-powered lawyer than a Department of Supernatural Entities agent, but since they had been visiting some individuals in the financial district, it had actually been appropriate.

"Rules are there to keep everything working smoothly. And they are following the rules," Mika chided, shifting his feet a little. New shoes were always a pain to break in, and a day of walking in dress shoes had left his soles aching and a new blister forming.

She lowered her voice a little, glancing sideways at the mundanes around them. "Foreseeing stock exchange dips and rises, mind reading and fortune telling is following the rules?"

"For them, yes."

"It's unfair. How is the average mortal supposed to compete against that?" she snapped.

"For one thing, it's no worse than having sophisticated software making millions of trades a second to eke out a tiny, tiny margin over and over again. Your average citizen doesn't have access to that either, do they? They also don't have billions of dollars lent to them so they can short a stock and make millions, making legitimate businesses unable to raise capital no matter how sound their fundamentals," Mika said, patiently. "I could go on. The market isn't fair. Never has been. And don't look so surprised. I know a few things."

Ophelia Eliades snapped her jaw shut, though a touch of surprise still lingered in those green eyes.

"Anyway, would you cripple our country when everyone else is doing the same?" Mika sighed. "They've been dabbling in finance ever since the first public—or private—corporation came into being. Some of the biggest changes in our world have been driven—or financed—by them.

"Remember. Our job isn't to govern our other natural brethren. It's to watch, caution and curtail excesses. They self-govern for the most part."

"Foxes and hen houses."

"If they step out of line, the government will deal with them. You have to stop thinking of them as private citizens, but more as individuals with a kind of diplomatic immunity," Mika said. "Not all of them, of course. But for our cases? The ones we deal with? Certainly. Our subjects are exceptional, so we keep a closer eye on them all and smooth over situations when mundane and magical meet."

O pursed her lips, staring up at the brick wall. Turned her head to the side, toward the crowd that waited in the alleyway, thankfully one not filled with dumpsters. Grumbled. "Like making sure paperwork for the building is appropriately filed, eh?"

"Would you rather that he not cook?" Now, that was a question that stumped O. She looked concerned, not just for the disappearance of the restaurant itself but the implications. Not that Mika was going to let it end there, continuing to lecture his new partner. "If Mo Meng weren't here, where —else—what else—would he be doing? Running around like a rogue jinni, causing headaches wherever he went?"

"I get the point. But he's not that powerful...."

"No. Almost no one else is," Mika said, holding the door open for a pair who exited, the two short customers flickering before his eyes for a moment as reality warred with glamour. The box by his belt vibrated a little, though he ignored it as he stepped in, head of the line at last.

Only to be surprised by the new greeter, recognition sparking. O's mouth hung open, black eyes locked on the well-dressed, handsome young man before her bearing a familiar clipboard.

"Name? Party of two?" his voice was deep, cultured and snooty.

"Uhh... Mika. We actually have—"

"We do not take reservations. You will have to wait like all the others," the boy promptly cut him off. Eyes drifted down and up, taking in their suits. A slight nod as though he approved of their clothing. "Currently, we're expecting about a thirty-minute wait." He lowered his voice, muttering to himself.

"It'd be faster, if some people actually ate, rather than chatted."

"But we're not..." O tried, only to subside at the withering look sent her way.

"Actually, we're here to meet some friends," Mika offered brightly, ignoring the glare sent at him. His gaze swept over the group, noted Jotun by himself and pointed. "Our party is right there."

As though he could tell it was a lie, the boy sniffed, but he did step aside. There was a tiny smile of mischief tugging at his lips, as though he approved of their deception.

Gripping O's arm firmly, Mika hurried down the stairs, leaving the boy to his job behind them. O followed mutely, breaking free of her surprise after they were halfway there and whispering.

"Do you know who that is...?"

"Yes. It's just his son, it's fine..."

"Fine...!" She hissed. "But...!"

"It's *fine*." Mika plastered a bright smile on his face as he reached Jotun. "Clan Chief, Master of the Forge... I was wondering..."

"I heard," Jotun rumbled. "Inviting yourself to my table. Typical of your agency..."

O quailed a little at the look while Mika soldiered on with a smile. "We're just here to get dinner. Surely you wouldn't deny us that? After all, the generosity of your table is well known..."

"My table?" Jotun hummed to himself, then a smile appeared as his gaze drifted over to Tobias beside him, the pile of plates before them already growing. "No, no. It is your table, that I was here for. Early."

"Our ... table." Mika slowly repeated the words. His gaze followed theirs to the table, already wincing at the expected expense report and the explanation he would have to make. More paperwork. "Yes, of course. Our table."

Tobias offered a thumbs-up to the big man as he shifted his seat, kicking with one stubby leg at a chair as an invitation to the dumbfounded O.

The woman took it disconsolately, leaning over to whisper to Mika once she was seated. "Following the rules, are we?"

"Rules can be bent, when needs must," Mika said, primly; a hand raised to catch Kelly's attention. "So, what are we eating...?"

Fifteen
The Dirty Past

"Such small servings," Professor Southeil muttered, using her fork to push around chopped pork rib shorts in the small bowl, watching the liquid that had gathered at the sides shift. "And what are these black things? Beetles?"

"Black beans. Fermented," Marilyn said, the upper edge of her chopsticks coming into contact with Ursula's fork and pushing it aside a little. "Don't poke at the food unless you intend to take it. That's so unhygienic!"

"Gone native, I see," Ursula sniffed, but then adroitly dodged the next attempt by Marilyn to push her fork aside by just not being where Marilyn's chopstick was going to be. That caused a small frown to appear on the elegant woman's face, one that Ursula ignored as she speared a piece of meat. "And you can go back to eating eggplant. I'll take this…"

"As if! You're not taking the whole dish," Marilyn said, darting in so quickly that Ursula could not stop her from snagging a rib end and bringing it back to her plate. Little droplets of oil and pork juices fell onto the table as she did so, the meat glistening palely.

"Mpphfff—!" was Ursula's answer. She was too busy chewing on the rib, spitting the small bone out onto her fork expertly as she savored the taste. The fermented black beans added umami to the simple dish, ginger laid on the sides to give the meat a bite. Wine—not the grape wine that Ursula was all too familiar with, but the more subtle flavor of rice wine—broke down the meat a little, gave the pork another layer of flavor. The pork itself was rich, a little fatty but also meaty in a way that she had not experienced in ages. She let out a little moan, the very intensity of flavor pulling the noise from deep in her belly.

"Nearly as good as good sex…"

Marilyn grinned in reply, even as Ursula looked around, searching for the waitress or the boy to answer her question. With the pair busy at the opposite ends of the restaurant, she was left only with her dining companion. A companion who was tucking in to another piece of meat, and so, rather than be left in the dark—and oh, she so hated that—Ursula reached out with a touch of her own gift.

Not to look forward. That way was always pain and regret and frustration. Who wanted to know the future, when so much of it would never come true and even more could never be changed? Only overweening fools like the wannabe-immortals imagined themselves the Atlases of existence, able to make the future dance to their disharmonious tunes.

As though history and events were a dog to be trained, content to follow along at every command.

History—and the future—had numerous influences. A single pebble might start a landslide, but finding the pebble and the right mountain was never that simple. The river of time and events flowed without end, and though might one dam one particular course, sooner or later, all dams broke.

Just ask the jinn.

Even so, men and women and gods tried, over and over again. It was the seductive lure of foretelling, because just maybe, this time it would be different. That your warnings would not go unheard, that events would play out well and that you had not made it worse, somehow. The harsh truth was that the future could only be changed by the present, not by looking ever forward.

No, she did not look to the future, but to the past.

Images of the meat boiling and further back, being prepared. Frozen, butchered, drained in a farm. The creature that it came from...

"Boar!" she cried, surprised. Then, not so much, when she thought of it. Well fed, cared for on a small farm, the taste and intensity of wild boar—not truly wild, of course—would always be more intense than the simple domesticated pig, no matter how well cared for. The untamed variant of the porcine was what gave this shard of rib its deeper taste.

"Boar!?" Marilyn asked, elegant eyebrow rising in query.

Only to be ignored as the fork darted over, piercing a piece before depositing itself in the mouth. Ginger and cloves, a touch of five-spice and rice wine all mixed together with the fermented black beans, the entire dish steamed for hours to offer an intense but subtle flavor. Slow-cooked for hours in the heat to allow the meat to pull away from the bone, so that only a little prodding was required by her tongue.

She spat the bone out, chewed on the meat that was still bouncy, requiring her to process the entire thing between her teeth. More juices deposited in her mouth as she masticated it, the slight burn of the rice wine and ginger and then, it was over. Leaving –her—her mouth—empty, in a way that only another piece could fill.

"You are right," Marilyn muttered. "He's using boar. Must be leftovers from the other day... Quite pleasant really, though unexpected."

"Unexpected. Delightful, you mean! " A hand reached sideways without looking, snagging Kelly as she stepped pass. "One more!"

"Certainly." Kelly looked down pointedly at the hand holding her, then tugged it free with a gentle yank. Ursula blushed, ducking her head.

"Sorry, dear! I got excited. Forgot my ... current manners."

"Current?"

"You'd be surprised what changes, over the years," Marilyn supplied. "It's hard work, remembering what is normal now and keeping up to date. Was a time, not so long ago, that we wouldn't be allowed to sit here, by ourselves. Not without some form of acceptable companionship." A slight tilt of her head to take in Ursula. "Well, some of us at least." Ignoring the dangerous glare her chewing companion shot her, the svelte raven-haired beauty added, "Never mind, of course, the ever-changing vocabulary."

"Though you can often draw understanding from context. Temperature changes are often –good—or bad. Exclamations from tone of voice. Made-up words are often nonsense that can be ignored," Ursula said. "And, of course, you can just mark them down if they use it in their papers."

"Still insisting on educating young women, are you?" Marilyn said.

"Better than training them to spread their legs."

"Oh, you do that later. First, you make them enamored with you." Red lips curling up, as Marilyn continued. "My skills never go to waste, no matter the age."

"What's the point, when the space between their ears is emptier than the space where your heart should be!"

They barely noticed as Kelly left, murmuring reassurances of adding a second order of the short ribs, carrying empty plates and bowls as she left. Too caught up in their bickering, rehashing old arguments and even older events.

For a moment, as the young woman swept by with another bowl, Ursula considered pilfering the dish. Maybe forcing the recipient to hand it over to her. After all, it was just those foolish government agents. At least they'd moved on from their desire to control the future.

She remembered, all too well, when their department was more than just observers. More than just silent watchers. The quiet battles that had been waged to change their minds, to allow the tides of history and progress to flow.

No, she remembered a past that was all too close, and a future that was but a single decision, a single election away. If...

But that was the allure of the future, wasn't it? That it could always be anything you wanted it to be.

If.

"Did you know that we have a pair of suits here?" Damian asked Kelly as he hurried over to the pass, plates and bowls stacked high in his hands.

"Of course. They're here once a week at least," Kelly said. "I see they invited themselves to join Jotun and Tobias."

"Yes." Damian frowned. "I was sure the Clan Head would reject them."

"Jotun's quite nice, really," Kelly said. "At worst, he'd ask them to leave. Some of our other regulars might refuse, but most won't. No one wants to risk being thrown out." She smiled a little at the dwarf who was working his way through the plate before him, carefully. Everything artfully arranged in perfect alignment, the others at the table frustrated as they waited for the signal to eat.

"Why are we letting them in? You know what they do!"

"I do. More than you, boy. In here, all are treated equally," Mo Meng said, interrupting the pair as he dropped a set of plates at their pass. "No matter their origin, or their background. If you come to eat, you are the same to me." A slight wrinkling of his nose, as he turned to Kelly. "Except for those with allergies. They are allergies, right?"

Damian frowned even as Kelly's gaze drifted to the order sheet she had pinned most recently. "That's what they told me."

"Then there's only three or four dishes I can serve them." Mo Meng frowned. "I'll have to check. And you should inform them that the chance of cross-contamination is high. Today's not a day where I have been tracking things well." Now he looked troubled, as he glanced into the kitchen where more pots bubbled and the usual spotless kitchen was stained with spilled gravy and burnt pieces. "Things got out of hand."

"I could..." Damian opened his mouth, raising a hand. It was a simple charm, after all, an inversion of a familiar glyph. It would not even be that hard, though the result might sting a little.

"No. I'll deal with it. You get the dishes washed. We're running out of small bowls," Mo Meng said, cutting off his offer. "No magic in the kitchen."

"It's for a good cause," Kelly said.

"You're already using some!"

"We don't take shortcuts that don't need to be taken." Another firm shake of his head, before Mo Meng left to return to his kitchen.

Damian frowned, upset at being turned down. A part of him hungered to wield his magic, to cast the spell and break the man's rules—the mulish, angry portion that was never going to be okay with being told no. After all, who was the chef to tell him no? Did he not know who he was? Whose son he was?

He clamped down on his feelings, letting out a loud huff as he dispersed his anger. A small snort of smoke escaped his nostrils as he did so, causing Kelly to stare. He grabbed the big dish pan, ignoring the unasked question, refusing to acknowledge it.

Instead, he focused on his job.

His job.

That was the reason he was here, after all. To have a job.

Earn some money.

Learn some humility, maybe.

Rising to the Challenge

R oti warmed up, the simple egg-slathered piece of rolled carbohydrates was on its way out of the kitchen. A list of allergies a hand long, including everything from gluten to strawberries to various nuts, had arrived as well. A pain to work with, and on another day, Mo Meng would have seen it as a challenge to rise to. He might have tried something new, created a new dish from what he had on hand.

Today was not the day. There was too much chance of cross-contamination, too little care taken, except for the major allergies, to follow the line of thought. Instead, he regarded his workstations, fished out new pots and pans as he considered what else to make or what could be used in a dish for his patron.

The garlic smashed potatoes were fine. Nothing in there to worry about, though it was lucky he had not chosen to make any mashed potatoes today. Dairy, not surprisingly, was on the list of allergens passed to him.

Nothing deep fried or using the current batch of oil. Too much chance of cross-contamination. Luckily, he had a variety of oils that weren't peanut oil—not that he used that very often these days—and so it was just a matter of locating the right ingredients.

Good thing he had prepped the wings earlier in the day. Just a single large bag, left over from the butcher shop. Trimmed and cleaned, then mixed with a dry spice rub. Mo Meng preferred dry rubs – it made for less mess on the eating side, and less work on his. You could always add a sauce or glaze later, and when he was feeling extra enthusiastic that day or trying to layer the eating experience with multiple flavors, he did.

Today, though, with so many small dishes, a dry spice rub was perfect. He had pulled from his stores, going by feel rather than any specific ratios—smoked paprika as the base, sugar and brown sugar, garlic and onion powder, a touch of cumin and crushed fennel and a small dash of chili powder. Add in salt and oregano flakes, blend it all together to get a nice and consistent rub, and then throw in the metal pan and mix with the meat which had been dried beforehand.

The drying of the meat was an easy thing to miss, but doing so allowed more of the rub onto the meat, made sure it did not clot up, and when the entire tray of wings was later slipped into the oven, allowed the wings to bake and crisp up faster and more consistently. If you had the time, trimming any extra edges of skin and flesh helped reduce fattiness too.

He made sure to turn on a timer for ten minutes, just long enough for the wings to cook on one side before they were flipped over. You wanted to do that, to get a good even crispiness on both sides, though the convection oven helped a lot with that too. Some people liked to thread the wings on a skewer, raising them off the pan to allow more consistent heating all around, a way to skip the flipping. It was prep work that added a small increase in consistency, but also had the negative of leaving the meat a little less moist, since the hole poked through allowed liquids to escape.

The chicken wings Mo Meng knew would be a hit, even if he had insufficient numbers for all of his clientele. Probably for the best, because while they were charging a consistent price for all the plates—to make life simpler for poor Kelly—it was one of the more expensive dishes to make.

Meat always was.

He could, if he wished, run the restaurant at a loss. Had, initially, when he had few customers and the dishes were made for their pleasure and his own. Nowadays, though, he used profitability and cost as a constraint, a way to force him to innovate. After all, if the mundanes could do it—why not he?

It was for this reason he also pulled out the eggplants. Diagonal slices along the fat purple plant to create ovular portions. He set them aside face-up on a series of paper towels, after which he added a dash of kosher salt to sweat out some of its bitterness.

While Mo Meng enjoyed the taste, for many of his customers it was a touch too intense. Part of cooking was learning and understanding the preferences of one's customers to better serve them. It was why good personal chefs altered even tried and true recipes for the families they served. Of course, running a restaurant, he had to go more for the common denominator.

Once he finished slicing all the eggplants he had, Mo Meng moved off to work on the rest of his dishes, returning only after twenty minutes to dab the eggplants dry and transfer them to a prepped sheet pan, one already sprayed down and greased. Olive oil brushed across the top of each of the eggplant rounds before another quick sprinkling of salt, and the entire thing went into an oven for twenty more minutes.

In the meantime, it was time to work on the topping. He would use a regular tomato sauce for half, but for those with a tomato allergy, he also had a green pesto sauce left over. In this case, the pesto sauce had been made from dandelion tops and basil.

Funny, how such a useful plant as the dandelion was called a weed, and now he had to grow his own just so that they weren't contaminated by pesticides. There was something there, about labels and the modern world, but it was a train of thought for another time and person.

Once the eggplant was extracted, he slathered it with the sauce and either normal or goat mozzarella. Finally it was time for the toppings, everything from leftover pineapple to spinach and mushrooms to slices of pepperoni or cooked sausage or ground and spiced beef.

Whatever was on hand, really, that he had small amounts of, that could go on top. One of the advantages of pizza, that you could throw in leftover ingredients and call it part of your creation process. Not that you would tell the customer, and you had to know what tastes went together, but it did make for an easy dish.

To finish it off, he slipped it back into the ovens to warm it all over, make sure not to cross-contaminate and have a couple of plates earmarked for the particular patron and keep moving. Grabbing finished ramekins full of soup, garlic potato plates, skewers of roasted vegetables and more.

It was as he arrived that he overheard Ursula causing more trouble…

"It was never a thing, you know," Ursula said.

"What wasn't?" Marilyn asked.

"Allergies. Sensitivities." Ursula sniffed. "People have gotten so much weaker, since we were young."

"Weaker? Or did those who have issues die off earlier?" Marilyn said. "Certainly, I recall fewer problems when we were growing up, but I also recall numerous plagues, diseases and even common colds laying low friends and family. Never mind what was considered medicine by the physicians of old. Leeching and bleeding…"

The pair of ladies shuddered in unison.

"Surely you don't think it's the people, as much as the environment?" Marilyn said. "I certainly have noticed the drop in magic, and we all know how that has an effect on life."

"A little of that, but have you seen them?" A nod over to Jotun, then Tobias. "In their prime, their leaders were lean and muscular and fit. Maybe a little unwashed, but well built. Now, there's still strength beneath all that, but there's a softness to them…"

"You mean fat," Marilyn said. From their respective seats, both of the aforementioned chunky pair glared at the girls. "And that's the point. People were thinner because they lacked enough food. Most didn't have enough—or if they did, it was because they took it from others. Even when there was a surplus, we had to can and store for the winter and early spring or watch it go to waste."

Ursula grunted. "But they were healthy. Moving. Traveling from place to place or working dawn to dusk. None of this sitting around, resting. Eating food that has so much processed sugar you could feed a family of four—if they didn't die from the lack of nutrition."

"You're going to next say how things were better, overall." Marilyn's nose wrinkled. "Except the largest cities were barely a million or two at most, most of them cesspools—literally—of bacteria and illness. I buried more than one lover early because of illness and simple injuries that if we had known how, could have been treated." Her nose wrinkled again as she added. "And the smell...!"

"I don't miss the smells, yes." Ursula chuckled. "Or mostly. It is nice to visit a farm, once in a while, or go riding. Not that I did much of the latter till later in life."

"Not ladylike. How did you handle the laws, blocking ownership of property or wealth?" Marilyn asked. "Certainly the colonies and England were horrendous for that. I just moved to places where they were a little more enlightened or made do with the right kind of husband."

"You weren't the only traveler, my dear." Ursula grinned. "I'll admit, I spent much of my time in Britain. But till recently, there was much land that was unclaimed. Or the owners were willing to look the other way, when the occupier was suitably useful."

Marilyn's voice dropped. "Working as a cut witch?"

"Sometimes."

Now the pair were grim-faced, recalling older, messier times. Times when being women—even ones with gifts—was harder, when basic rights like having a say about their future, or owning property or where one lived was but a dream for most. Not all places, not all countries; but so many…

It was why, for all her cutting words, Ursula understood her table companion, even admired the way she taught her new recruits how to manipulate others. The art of seduction and manipulation was a skill that had a long and necessary history.

"This new world isn't all bad. It just needs to cut down on the excess," Ursula said.

"At least we're not in the south. I hate traveling down there, so much added sugar you can taste it in *everything*. There's utterly no reason for it to be in baby formula."

"They don't stop you from traveling?" A slight indication of the head to the newcomers, the pair of DESE agents seated a short distance away.

"Actually make it easier, if you're willing to work with them." Marilyn grinned. "Private flights, passport officers that know what's up and work late. They even used to have the right stamps, all of it handled quickly and efficiently."

"You don't worry about them tracking you?"

"Do you carry a 'smart' phone?"

"Yes."

"Then they're doing it already."

Ursula grunted. "Not mine."

Marilyn dropped her voice again. "Enchantment?"

"Yes. Lily's boy showed me how. Interesting young man, though a little naïve." At the question, she elaborated. "They came for tea a few months ago."

"So it was him who showed it to you? Not her?"

"She says he's better. Something about understanding the underlying concept of microcircuitry and telephone networks." A shrug. "Lily tried to explain her own attempts at using Faraday cages, but it just blocked the phone from working entirely," Ursula said the last sentence as though she was parroting words. "It's a little out of my area of expertise. Hard enough to keep up in my areas of interest. I'll leave the rest to others."

An elegant, painted finger came up to tap herself on the lips. "Well, I might have to talk to him, next time he's in town."

"You should. Fascinating young lad, but do keep your hooks out of him," Ursula said. "Unless you want to be dragged into more messes."

"A child of chaos, that one?"

"He's Lily's apprentice." As though that was enough.

Which, when Marilyn considered it, it was. After all, the lady was the precursor of chaos and change.

She only had to look around at her once quiet restaurant for the supernatural, now a bustling hotspot that even the mundane visited.

Child of change and chaos for sure.

Seventeen
Battling Chaos

Chaos. An undying enemy a kitchen always battled, and in turn, the restaurant as a whole. No matter how hard you worked, entropy sought to sink its claws in every evening, finding the soft spots, the places of weakness where experience and personality and systems were found lacking.

Where, if you turned away for too long, dishes burned, plates broke, and tempers frayed.

Magic, for all its wonder and miracle making, was an agent of chaos in itself. Though some might seek to pin down magic to its component parts, to utilize formulas and equations to understand its fundamental forces, for Mo Meng, it was an art form. Much like cooking, each spell was a twisting, changing recipe. One that could be modified based on dozens of factors to suit one's needs.

Rice—the simplest dish to make. A sushi chef in training was tasked with making rice for two years before they could graduate to further tasks. Two years, for a simple dish—and yet, in its deceptive simplicity, the truth of skill and dedication and artistry was showcased.

New bags of rice, arriving every day. Grown in different parts of the field, different altitudes and heights, watered and processed at different times. Some a touch starchier than others, others more waterlogged and dirty. Weevils had to be removed, excess starch washed off, different kinds of water—and water temperatures—utilized in the process.

Then, steaming, at the right temperature, for the right amount of time. Utilizing stock or plain water or coconut milk, all to add another layer of taste.

Even the process of cooking was a question, whether to use a machine or do it yourself, over the fire or an electric heater, carefully gauging when the water came to a boil and it was time to lower the temperature and allow the rice time to cook. When to remove the cover, how long to leave it on.

Different levels of doneness depending on the final use of the rice.

After which you had to fluff the rice, breaking it up and releasing excess moisture via trapped steam. Once done, additional simple ingredients could be –added—garlic or butter or soy sauce, toppings from furikake to garlic chips, or perhaps one would soak the rice in tea.

A hundred different dishes, all from the same base.

Magic was like that—the ingredients might seem the same at the base, but it changed too, when one paid enough attention. When one cared to pay attention to see the difference between one emotion, one flavor of power and another.

Mixing and matching, so that the spell or dish altered each and every time. Making the most of what you had, but always different. Always a new variable that couldn't be accounted for in the basic spell, that had to be managed and that a craftsperson had to rein in from devolving into chaos. Choose not to add new employees, choose to make dishes one knew, choose to avoid casting magic on the dishes, or else you added another variable.

Chaos and order. Two sides of a teeter-totter: press down too hard on one side to control it and sooner or later, it would spring back. Perhaps wisdom was in finding the joy in bouncing between the two poles like a child falling and rising, laughing in delight at the giddy heights and falls.

Perhaps he had leaned too far into a world of order. Justified his choice to not use magic after centuries of indulging in it. Until, that was, the situation became untenable and it was necessary to not only have a single employee but two. When knowledge of his restaurant had become public, and even the spells utilized to hide it could no longer contend with the weight of modern technology.

Social media, the world wide web, maps and word of mouth, there was only so much that wards of ignorance and memory loss could do.

Now, Mo Meng fought a losing battle against chaos and unpredictability, where systems and routine were insufficient for the volume of commerce he dealt with. Chaos crept in between the cracks, and sank its claws deep.

There, Damian stumbled, searching through restaurant drawers and the closet for additional washing liquid and a drying cloth. Hunting for additional plates and utensils and napkins, even as Kelly hurried from one patron to another, order slips dashing and a strained smile on her lips.

Burgeoning chaos, lurking in thinned lips and red, flushed skin. Jerky movements as an ego was threatened, as a fuse was lit and threatened to erupt.

Mo Meng drifted over, a quartet of plates stacked on two hands as he made his way to the pass. Never pausing as he threw some water on the burgeoning blaze. "Two down, one up for the spare utensils. Washed dishware should go into the dryer. The first batch should be dry now."

He watched the boy freeze out of the corner of his eyes, visibly struggling with the aid. Then, after a too long hesitation, he moved to follow directions. Not a single word of thanks, but Mo Meng had not expected one.

Dampening the chaos, plucking a pot from the stove top.

He would have to do it again, soon.

That was life—a repetition of tasks, over and over again.

The trick was learning to enjoy the repetition.

Dropping recently cleaned and dried warm plates and a half dozen bowls in their resting spots, Damian finished emptying the dishwasher. Warm plates, almost burning hot, didn't bother him at all. He always liked the heat. Nostrils flared as he breathed in, three short sharp breaths before a longer exhalation.

Doing so reminded him, and he glanced to the side at the quarter-empty waste bin. Wondering if his employer made use of it, or, perhaps more importantly—how.

Did it go into compost piles? Or get picked up by gremlins and knockers, the sporelings and mycelian who reveled in the waste and refuse of others? His father had a number of deals with such creatures, or so he was told. Much less known than his workday arrangements with imps and nickars and the like.

Not that he had much contact with father dearest. Not when he was one of a dozen different sons and daughters, all set to grow up and bring about chaos and maybe, if they did it right, fulfil a prophecy.

He was nearly as bad as the Olympian.

Nearly.

Creaking and screeching made Damian look down; the handful of cutlery in his hand was bent, the grips twisted and some beginning to melt. Looking around quickly to see who might have noticed, he caught Professor Southeil's gaze. A pair of all too knowing eyes.

He felt his heartbeat speed up and his eyes narrowed. Vision threatened to disappear, even as the roaring in his ears increased, a portion of him screaming *how dare she think she knew him, just because she could see didn't mean she could understand and he definitely did not need her pity.*

"Don't worry, I broke a dozen plates my first week working as a waiter." Kelly tore an order slip from her booklet, adding it to the line of tickets waiting for Mo Meng. "Just toss them into recycling and clear table six."

"Six...?"

"Near the door."

Funny, how the bright smiling slip beside him, offering *him* sympathy, did not anger him further. Instead, he found himself turning to the recycling bin and doing as she said before grabbing a clean dish cloth, only slowing to ask, "Is it always like this?"

"This busy?" Kelly said. "Busier today than normal, but not by much compared to yesterday. Which was busier than the day before."

It wasn't what he meant, for his eyes drifted back to Professor Southeil, to Tobias and Jotun and then Marilyn. "Didn't you already have a wait list? How could you be busier?"

A wide smile was his only answer, as she breezed past him with more plates full of baked potatoes and vegetables for the guests.

Leaving him frustrated, but in a good way this time.

Eighteen
Drugs and Other Protection

Mika crossed his arms in front of him, watching his partner and the surroundings, a niggle of concern worrying at him. This job was not always suitable for all personalities, and the woman had entered the service with a strike against her already. Now, Ophelia stared at Marilyn and Ursula at their table, the pile of plates that they'd refuse service on growing with each moment. They competed over every dish, somehow managing to achieve a balance of what was consumed, even as one or the other leaned into favorites.

The clatter of a light plate took his attention from his partner, back to the new dishes that were arriving. He could worry about how she was handling Ursula's presence later. After all, technically he was off the clock—though like with most professions with added social responsibilities, he was never truly off.

He could, however, devote his focus to two things at once. A hand reached out, snatching one of the white, half-translucent spring rolls from the freshly deposited plate. Vermicelli, bright orange mango, fresh mint leaves, carrots and cucumbers glistened in the air beside him, fresh and succulent and disappearing into the peanut sauce bowl on the plate.

Mika dipped the roll into the dark brown peanut sauce, watching it coat the translucent white roll as he shook it over the bowl once and then again. A small smile appeared on his face as he breathed deep, the smell mingling with the other plate of deep-fried spring rolls .

No longer able to wait, he popped the whole thing into his mouth and took a bite. Rich, nutty sauce replete with umami from the peanut and soya sauce, combined with a generous helping of salt, filled his mouth. The peanut sauce overwhelmed the initial subtler flavors till he started chewing. Bouncy vermicelli gave way beneath his teeth, the thin rice noodles' light and delicate flavor mixing with the sauce, the mint a burst of coolness that filled his mouth. Then, the sweetness of the mango, the crunch of bean sprouts, the taste of fried egg.

Tempting, to dip once more into the peanut sauce.

Eyes glittering with mischief, he noted how Ophelia had snagged one of the crispy spring rolls and turned away to stare once more. A small smile lit his face, for what she did not know would not hurt her. Notwithstanding overly rigid moral –objections—or hygienic ones, which when you dealt with slime monsters, kelpie and gremlins as part of your day job was much less of a –concern—it was a minor sin.

Even so, Mika made sure to move quickly, taking the opportunity to double dip before her attention returned to their meal, barely containing a slight moan as the spring roll exploded in his mouth again with a rush of fresh and vibrant tastes reminiscent of early spring and a dip in a cold stream. He hadn't taken a holiday in ages, and now that winter had arrived, he wasn't sure when he might have time to do so. Something about the winter brought out the worst in his clients, it seemed.

At least Halloween was over. That was a pain and a half.

By the time O returned her attention to their table, he had finished the spring roll and was reaching for the crispy versions. This time around, she glared, swallowing quickly to blurt out:

"Fingers!" She pointed at the chopsticks beside them. "Use them."

"I am using my fingers," Mika said, impishly. Something about his rookie made him want to twit her. Probably because of her over-serious demeanor at times and complete naivete at others. It was one reason he didn't like having partners, especially because they made his job harder. "See?" Holding one of the fried spring rolls in hand, he waved it back and forth before dipping it into the sweet vinegar sauce with floating grated carrot pieces in it.

"Filthy..." Grimacing, she picked up a second roll—with her chopsticks—and raised it, quickly dipping hers in the same sauce before taking a bite. "You know that's how you spread germs around, right?"

"That's why I take my vitamins," Mika said. "And all the various tinctures and herbal remedies they shove down our throats."

Her nose wrinkled at that. "I don't understand how you can drink and eat all that. They either taste like mud mixed with gravel or ground up parts of beetles and insects tossed in bitter juice and the occasional dash of sour lemon."

"That's because..."

"NOPE! Not listening," O said, pushing a palm out. "I'm eating."

Of all the things she could have said to stop his teasing, that was the most effective. Mika had enough appreciation of the food and Mo Meng—never mind love for his life if he spoiled the meal for anyone else—to stop.

"Well, it's necessary. Don't think I haven't noticed you've been skipping out on taking your daily too," Mika said.

"Then why didn't you say so earlier?"

"I'm your partner, not your babysitter. You want to come down with a month's worth of the runs or a cold that lingers for three, that's your problem." Mika shrugged. "We all do that, eventually. Think we're smarter than the regulations. If not this, another one. You won't die, just wish you did."

"It's not that bad, surely?"

"You deal with dozens of species every week, each of which have their own sub-culture of food and diseases. Some of which include diseases that are mildly infectious. Since some of those species don't interact with the general populace, it isn't a problem. But we're poking our nose in their business and you expect it to work out well?"

"But it's just minor stuff, right?"

"Majority of the time, nothing jumps the barrier between species that's a real issue, but when it does..." Mika shrugged. "That's when it gets bad. And sure, the really nasty stuff we have our shamans and scientists on hand to deal with, but your average cold? That's a battle we lost long ago. On a global scale, it's a non-issue. Individually, though? When the species has four sets of nostrils and you only have two, then it's snot heaven."

"Doesn't sound like heaven."

"It is for the snot."

With that particular statement made, he bit into the roll with savage pleasure, crunching through the crispy outer shell. It cracked and little shards broke off, littering the plate he was eating over and his hand. Not that he paid much attention, not while chewing happily.

Unlike the fresh spring rolls, the deep fried ones were packed full of seasoned meat. Five-spice probably, soy sauce, salt, maybe some paprika and a touch of chili? The meat, too, was different, a mixture of pork and maybe chicken. Slightly fatty, very moist and somewhat sweet. There was also a secondary degree of texture, a little chewier than the crispiness of the initial fried spring roll wrap, that came from the onions and cabbage included in the roll. All of which left a heavily seasoned, savory taste lingering in his mouth.

Mika swallowed and then popped the undipped half into his mouth after noting O glaring at him. Without the sweet and sour vinegar dip that gave the initial shock, the savoriness and spice of the meat came through much more clearly, causing his saliva to flow faster. In seconds, he was done, the small spring roll consumed.

Leaving him with the question of which of the two he preferred—and which to take before his companion had an unfair share.

Nineteen
Bacon Wrapped Anything

The more things spun out of control, the faster the boy moved. Kelly kept an eye on Damian as he dashed around the restaurant with dirty plates and glasses, pouring water and cleaning tables with swift efficiency. After it had been explained what his basic job was, he seemed to have picked up on his duties and was fulfilling them with minimal fuss.

Not that it was very complicated, once you got down to it. On the other hand, the little bit of flair that he had been adding to the process was a thing of beauty in itself. Everything from the way he picked up the plates, sweeping them off with a scoop of his hands, to the toss and bounce of glasses from his hand as he laid a table added a touch of flair to a job that was often pedestrian. It was unnecessary but certainly fun, though a little intimidating for Kelly.

She would have worried about the plates and utensils, about what kind of destruction and damage he might do, if not for the slight swirl of –light—flares of scarlet and ivory, of crimson and black that appeared at the edges of his movements. It was there and gone so fast that you might think you'd imagined it; if you were a mundane. A trick of the light that helped shift a glass a quarter of an inch to the right or protected a plate as it banged against the edge of the door as he swept through on tiptoe, spinning around like a black and white top.

Magic, chaotic magic, that flared and shifted and set the glyphs and –runes—and if there was a difference, she had yet to learn it—along ceiling beams and down columns, causing them to sparkle and flicker with energies of their own. Dancing in a way that was new and unusual.

It was as she stood by the pass, delaying just a touch for her boss to swing by with more orders, that she asked. "Is it okay?"

"I'm keeping up, though we're running out."

"No, I meant Damian. His ... magic?" She wasn't even sure it was magic, but it was the word she had to use. Some things, like a vampire's strength or a werewolf's hairiness, were just innate. Like the way magicians always arrived when dinner was being served or the fae's patronage of successful artists, though how one defined success was best left –unargued—it was just part of their makeup.

"It's being contained." He nodded to where Professor Southeil and Marilyn continued to converse, heads close together. "Ursula's always been good at being where she's needed." He frowned then, a surprising amount of emotion from her boss as he added. "Not always where she's needed most, mind you."

"Boss?"

"Not the time. You got tables and I got food on the grill." Then he was gone, back into the kitchen, leaving her wondering what that had been about. An annoying amount of information was left unsaid in this restaurant, history and unspoken social contracts so deep that an unsuspecting swimmer might find themselves dragged below by an overenthusiastic kelpie or two who'd invited you to go swimming in the lake, late at night.

Just as an example.

Back out, with the fresh plates, a glance downwards to check the order over. One of everything was one of everything, which meant that the table filled with Jotun and Tobias and the agents received theirs first. Tobias just grunted, focused as he was on eating, carefully and methodically, through the pile. Other than his refusal to let them take the plates piling up by the side, he had barely spoken since his arrival. Hard to talk when the dishes kept arriving and one was a slow eater.

She barely heard the thanks, the social niceties a common drone by this point. Jotun, however, rested a pair of fingers, wide and broad and surprisingly soft, on her wrist as she began to back off.

"Best leave those two alone." A small gesture to Damian and then Professor Southeil, tracking one and then the other across the floor. "Their kind always have had a connection." A glance at Marilyn, then he added, "Marilyn too, though of a different kind. She knows better than to involve you, and her depths are less ... chaotic."

"Really?"

"Just let them work it out. Nothing good ever comes of a mundane involving themselves." A slight frown. "Or even most others."

Deep waters. Which reminded her... "Water?"

"Yes, please."

"What is it with the Canadian fascination with maple syrup and bacon?" Ursula said, staring at the small dish, replete with various grilled and baked items all doused in the aforementioned liquid. Before she could pronounce further on the matter, Marilyn snatched up the only bacon-wrapped scallop piece, one that had been sliced apart, stuffed with crab—or perhaps faux-crab—and skewered by a small toothpick. "You many-tongued harlot!"

"Sticks and stones..." Mouth full of scallop, Marilyn somehow still kept it elegant.

"Pretty sure a stick is exactly what you need."

"You almost make me think you don't like me..."

Realizing what Marilyn was up to, Ursula snatched the first of the baked items, frowning a little when she realized it was a red pepper and cheese combination, all wrapped in, well—maple syrup bacon. However, unlike the majority of store-bought versions of the meat, this one was either purchased from a butcher or made directly by Mo Meng. Among other things, the slices were at least three to four millimeters thick, the ratio of fat and meat leaning more towards the meat side, and the entire morsel glistening with caramelized sugar from the maple syrup it had been soaked in.

A quick bite and she had to admit, there was something to the combination. Underneath the crunchy sweetness of the burnt maple sugar was the thick, chewy fattiness of the scallops and then the smoked cream cheese with a surprising dash of heat. Chili flakes had been embedded in the cheese, with enough spice that she found herself blowing out through her mouth in a desperate attempt to quench it, even as her cheeks flushed and pupils dilated.

"Too much!" Even as she complained, though, she was taking another bite, swallowing the last of the ingredients. Now that she was growing accustomed to it, she felt the mild crunch of the fresh red pepper, the tang and sweetness of the roasted vegetable.

"Weak!"

Ursula noted, however, that Marilyn avoided the pieces with cream cheese in them. Looking around, she spotted the capering busboy, and a thought crossed her mind. A hand rose, waving him over. As he refilled her water glass with the pitcher that he managed to pull from who knew where, she twitched one hand in a series of signs.

A single glance downwards, before his gaze came up and Damian intoned, "No."

"Come now, it's a decent deal."

"No," Damian said. "I'm not doing that."

"Really?" She waggled the same free hand, crossing and twisting her fingers even as she casually blocked Marilyn with her other hand and stole the last, non-cheese-stuffed bacon-wrapped appetizer. "Because I'd say you need it."

"I'm not like my family."

A small, smirking smile, a glance down at his torso, flicking past the apron and the clothing and then upwards to the glowering face. "Of course you're not. You just think about it; okay, my dear?"

"I don't need to."

"Of course you do."

An angry snort. He spun away in moments, to refill a water glass at the table behind, and then moved on, trailing all the way to Tobias and the others, including a glowering O. Behind them, a rather frustrated man banged on his camera, tapping it from side to side and surreptitiously looking around for a free plug to utilize, the sprawl of electronics meant to tape his show shoved haphazardly into the bag beneath his feet.

"What was that all about?" Marilyn asked.

"Just a little business."

"I sometimes wonder which of you two is worse."

"We never make deals that aren't wanted, you know that, yes?"

"Doesn't make them good deals. People don't always know what is best for them."

"Like you?"

A slight inclination of the head. "Some deals last longer than expected and have unexpected consequences."

"Well, this is between the two of us, you know." A nod to the boy who swept up a new plate, ignoring a customer who had intended to scoop up the last shreds of melted butter with bread as he spun away. Somehow, though, moments later, the bread was coated in butter, dripping down it. "He needs it, and it should be fine, no?"

Marilyn chose not to answer. Like Jotun, she knew when it was time to back away. Instead she braved the final piece of bacon-wrapped asparagus and scallops. After all, bacon-wrapped anything was still a pleasure, no matter how much it was used.

TWENTY
Simple Salads

"The nerve of that woman!" The crash of a plate into the dishwasher caught Mo Meng out, causing him to glance to the side. Just as surprising was the sudden flare of chaos magic, just enough to keep the pair of plates from breaking and chipping.

Of course, the emerging chaos and entropic magic had to go somewhere. He could feel his enchantments strain further, drawing the uncontrolled energy upwards before it could cause damage beyond a slightly charred pancake and an overly soggy piece of bread in his soup. A small price to pay, considering what uncontrolled magic of that sort could do.

No one needed another flood.

"Take care in the present, watch your movements and actions." Lowering his voice a little as he placed the burned pancake and the ramekin of soup aside for his own snacking later, Mo Meng continued. "Your magic, too."

"There's too much work to do it mundanely."

"Not if you actually take the time to learn your job." He nodded to where Kelly breezed among the tables, a smile on her face, her steps quick and efficient but never seeming rushed. If not for the slight air of frantic energy that was part of her demeanor, one might not even notice the pressure she was under keeping up with the packed tables.

"Are you sure she's a mundane?"

"Yes. Can't you tell with those eyes of yours?" An eyebrow rose, for he'd noticed the edging of red around the pupils, the way they glinted and burned as the night went along.

"They don't work that way. What it tells me, though, is that she's everything that she seems—and more. Much more, considering her past."

"Strength comes from testing and from the trials that we face. There is no growth without pressure, no change without heat. You should know that most of all." With the boy calmed and disposing of the scant leftovers properly and putting his plates away, Mo Meng returned to his own pots and pans, to the grill with the last few items that needed grilling.

"Her family, yes?" Damian said, uncertainly.

"Biological, yes." At his frown, Mo Meng shrugged. "It's complicated. I haven't asked much."

"Why?"

"Why would I? She will tell me when she's ready. Or not. Her past is unlikely to cause trouble in the restaurant or affect the patrons or the city."

The boy grimaced, hands empty, hovering over the dishwasher. He stared at them, the dark-colored nails, the edged tips, the dark bare skin revealed beneath his rolled-up shirt sleeves. Muttered after a moment, "I don't want any of this."

"Then why not take her up on the offer?"

"You heard."

"I guessed. It's not complicated, when you put two of your kind together. Like a pair of magnets, sitting not far from one another." Mo Meng finished plating another series of small plates, scooping up a trio and gesturing. "Help me put these on the pass."

"I'm more than just my heritage."

"Then make a choice. Or don't." Mo Meng clicked his tongue. "But get the plates on the pass. We have guests to serve."

Chivvied into motion, Damian walked over to help the chef who had already abandoned his post to care for more of his dishes, a stack of new metal containers sitting nearby, the smell of vinegar filtering through the air from one, clean meat from another.

Just more plates that needed to be served, a never-ending parade of tiny dishes, as though the chef was challenging his patrons to see who dropped first.

Mo Meng checked on the pickled radishes first. They sat in the same container as the other pickled vegetables, all of them using the same pickling sauce, though the other side was filled with shredded carrots, cucumbers, onions and other scraps.

The radishes, on the other hand, were perfectly cubed, created weeks ago for a planned fried chicken night that had been delayed, and then forgotten about. Sugar, vinegar, sea salt. Simple enough to start, but the question was always the ratio, the mixing and variation to reach the optimal levels for both the radishes—which had their own natural sweetness—and the ingredients used.

After a quick sampling to verify that it had not, for some reason, gone bad, Mo Meng was ladling small portions of pickled vegetables onto plates. Something sweet, something refreshing, on the other side, the rest of the vegetables with their own crunch and sweetness and spice to play against the other dishes served which might have been a little too heavy or oily.

Variety was the spice of life or his dishes, after all.

Even as he worked, his mind spun through the rest of his ingredients, through what else he had left. There was not much, not if he intended to cook for tomorrow and the day after. Going shopping for the next day's ingredients would be annoying enough without tapping into his existing stores.

Still, he wasn't done, not yet.

The only question was whether the boy and Ursula would get themselves sorted in time.

In the meantime, he had another dish to finish. Popcorn chicken—made from the remnant pieces of skin, fat and other leftovers from trimmed chicken pieces that had been marinating in the other container overnight, soaking in buttermilk and spices. Now, he fished the portions out with a strainer, piling them in a single layer on wire mesh grills to drip dry.

He moved fast, rotating between the various trays till his container was empty. Setting aside the now empty container of leftover marinade, he prepped the flour covering with a dash of paprika, more salt and pepper and a little cumin. Mix it all together, toss the dried chicken pieces in it and then transfer to the nearby deep fryer, egg wash and final preparations. Everything needed to be ready to go, for you could not delay too long once the wet wash had contacted the flour, or the entire mixture grew gummy, hard and clumpy in the end. Piece after piece was dumped into the flour, case of egg wash, panko bread crumbs, and then straight into the deep fryer basket.

A quick engagement of a timer just so that he didn't forget, and he was off, back to dealing with other dishes that were on the verge of burning. In a few cases, he noted, things were cooked a little over the optimal amount of time; often a minute or two longer than was optimal.

Most wouldn't notice, though he expected a few complaints. At some point, he'd need to find additional help. There was only so much that even he, experienced and knowledgeable as he might be, could do. Not with the volume of orders.

The question still remained, who he'd trust in his kitchen. Few people realized how much additional work it was working with others, or how often added help did not double the throughput but often less. Sometimes much less, if you had the wrong person.

Certainly in the beginning, when the newcomer was learning the ropes. Once he tried to find someone who could handle all that needed to be learned.

Deep thoughts as he worked his ramekins, scraping out the last of the soup and adding cheese and bread before popping the entire thing into the oven, withdrawing the last of the baked chicken wings and baked potatoes.

Once the timer went off, it was time to extract the basket, leave it on top to drip dry while another basket of drenched and dredged chicken bits was added to the fryer on the other side. Not particularly challenging food, but it had the advantage of being generally well received and easy to make.

Which, when you had a half dozen dishes on the go, was important.

Sometimes it wasn't about style, but effectiveness.

Now, the question was whether the pair would agree.

Twenty-One
Crunch and Crackle

"Do you think he's stressed?" Tobias said, staring at the latest pair of plates to arrive. He looked at them rather dubiously, the fried chicken pieces and the pickled salads, brows drawn so tight that the lines between his eyebrows and across the top of his face were starker.

"What? Because he's making simple and tasty food?" Jotun growled, spearing one of the pieces of fried chicken with his fork. "Is it too pedestrian for you?"

"You know I don't have a problem with that, or the fried mushrooms he came up with on the last dish. Or anything Mo Meng cooks, but it is a little…"

"Simple? Peasant food?"

Mika and O were watching the pair volley insults at one another, both of them knowing better than to get involved. Better to watch and enjoy their own plates. Not that either was eating much, not anymore, not after so many plates.

"Well, yes."

"Your purple blood is showing." Jotun grinned widely, popping the entire piece of chicken into his mouth and biting down with a hard and satisfying crunch. The crackle of crispy chicken skin and the shattering of the crispy fried egg, bread crumb and flour coating filled the surroundings, even as he reached the pieces of meat and skin beneath within moments, the moist juices released into his mouth.

"You know we don't have kings anymore."

"Could have fooled most of us, the way they treat you all."

"It was voted on." A shrug. "I can't stop the deep dwellers and mushroom eaters from doing what they will. It's better to keep them happy, to help them transition to a more egalitarian society, than to just abandon them."

"You don't have to explain yourself to me." Again the fork reached out, spearing a couple of chicken pieces and waving them around as he spoke. "It's not like you enjoy getting dressed up and paraded around the deep halls, right?"

"Exactly! Do you know how heavy those helmets are? Broken schist, they're built to withstand a collapse by themselves. Except, these days, half the enchantments don't work because there isn't enough Mana, so you have to hold the thing up on your shoulders and neck with sheer grit! The number of my ancestors with headaches and herniated necks and spine compressions—!"

"Sure, sure. Terrible headaches." All through the rant, Jotun kept answering his friend, his fork never halting as it speared the chicken pieces and slipped them into his mouth. It was only when the last piece was speared that Tobias realized what was happening.

"—you! That's my plate!"

"You can have the plate." Resolutely, the last piece of chicken was slipped into Jotun's mouth, a piece that consisted only of crispy chicken skin and breading, the extra loud crunch and crackle punctuating his words. Saliva exploded further into his mouth, the slight spice and taste of smoked paprika mixing with the black pepper and crisped skin to further the taste of fried loveliness. Jotun's eyes widened in pleasure and he let out an involuntary groan.

"You—!" Tobias glared. He looked over at Mika and O, who were polishing off the last pieces on their plate and returned his look angelically. Rather than complain further and lose out, he switched his attention to the still full plate of pickled radishes. He attacked it with a vengeance, even as his other hand rose and waved, trying to flag down Kelly before the restaurant ran out of the very popular dish.

"The thing you purple-bloods forget, there's always going to be more of us than you," Jotun said, winking at Damian who swung by with another plate of the chicken for Jotun. The boy grinned, a devilish smile on his lips as he ignored Tobias. A big hand dropped between plate and Tobias as a fork darted forward, even as he edged the plate over to the two agents. They, unashamedly, took pieces off the plate even as Tobias attempted to maneuver around the massive arm. "And this entire night is all about low food."

"It is not," Tobias snapped.

"Really? Because leftovers and scraps were what our people were forced to eat, when we were cast out." Jotun's voice rumbled, low and deep and filled with age-old hurt. "When they cleared us out of our lands, on their horses and steeds, with promises of death and retribution if we ever returned, those screaming ravens of death and their one-eyed master, we were forced to learn to eat whatever we could. Forced to work on their walls and take the meanest jobs, all because they felt they were better than us. Born of better stock."

Tobias lowered his fork, glancing away. Sometimes there was a reminder, a little comment that showed that for all of the dwarf's advanced age, the one beside him was older still. Millennia compared to his own centuries, a child to an adult.

Then, of course, the big man stole his food like a child and made him growl deep in his throat, as more of his pickled radishes disappeared even as he blocked any attempt at getting at the fried chicken.

Damian had paused for a moment in his never-ending spiral around the tables, head bent low to whisper to Professor Southeil. Marilyn should have been able to hear them; they were only a few feet away. One of the advantages, the increased senses of their kind—but she couldn't. Magic was in play, and it was chaos magic. The best and worst kind, because it could do everything and nothing at all; it just depended on how well you wielded it and how much destruction you were willing to leave behind.

Marilyn snagged another piece of fried chicken, watched as Damian stomped off again—gracefully still with a little pirouette—but angry, leaving Ursula alone. She waited for the woman to turn back before she leaned over, fork raised and waving to get her companion's attention.

"You are going to check over the contract, aren't you?"

"Now, why would I do that? I'm not some young sprout who's never done this before."

"He's not your average contractee."

"A little more robust, perhaps, but I can handle it."

"Can he?"

"Well, it's best for him to learn now, if he can't, don't you think?"

Now Marilyn rolled her eyes. "Taking advantage of the youth, are we stooping to that now?"

"Didn't we have this argument already?"

"A century or two ago, I believe. Just around when the suffragette movement began."

"I must admit, I'm rather proud of that one," Ursula said.

"You are not going to take credit for that," Marilyn growled. "There were dozens of us working in the shadows, pushing for a return to equality. Never mind the mundanes who were front and center of it all, who suffered for their beliefs and made it come true."

"Hah! You people, pushing from behind, not daring to do what was necessary. How many of the objectors did you deal with?" Ursula's nose wrinkled. "How many threads did you snip, just so that the tangle of fate could unwind like it was supposed to?"

"A little early, was it not?"

"Or entirely too late." Head lowered, a tight bun with just a sprinkling of dark hair left, graying and old. "How many did we lose, because we weren't willing to push faster?"

"You know they would never let us, not before then," Marilyn said. "I tried. We all did." Lips compressed, she added, "It's why I won't let you take advantage of him. We finally got the laws to work for us, to bring us to a place where justice can be found in more places than a protest in the streets or poison in the sheets."

"Who are you to do that?"

In answer, as Damian came by once more, Marily reached out and snagged his arm. As he stopped, she flicked her hand and a card appeared in it.

Marilyn de Rochefort

Barrister and Contract Lawyer

Beneath those words, visible to the mundane, another line started to appear, glowing golden and writing itself across the card as it interacted with his magic.

Lawyer at large for the supernatural

"What?" he said, turning the card over to reveal a simple logo, a pyramid with not an eye but smiling lips and just the hint of teeth. Sharp teeth.

"A dollar."

"What?" Again, he repeated himself.

"A dollar to engage my services. Discounted rate, only for tonight." Marilyn pointed a finger at Ursula. "And only because you're going to do a deal with this one."

"Speaking as though I'm a wicked stepmother or something," Ursula said, wrinkling her nose and making all the lines in her face deepen too.

"More like the witch in the forest in her gingerbread house."

"I am no child, you know," Damian growled at Marilyn. "My father would be rather upset if I engaged one of your kind without reading over the terms properly. We have quite a few of you below for a reason."

"No, child, certainly. But this is what I do. Can you say the same?"

Now Damian hesitated. "Still, to use you and not do it myself, he would be upset."

"Annoying your father? Sounds like a good reason to me, if I ever heard one."

He laughed and inclined his head. A hand dipped into his pocket, fishing around before emerging with a crisp hundred dollar bill. "All I have on me."

"It'll do." Snatching it from his hand, Marilyn turned to Ursula, a predator about to pounce on newfound prey. After all, there was more than one way to suck the life out of another.

TWENTY-TWO
Making Friends

Magic and food, food and magic. It swirled all through the restaurant, in the kitchen, among the patrons and staff. That was the trick of the restaurant, hiding the reality of the magic that surrounded them all, even if it should have been obvious. Kelly and the regulars understood—contributed, even. Even the mundanes sensed it, though only at the edges for the most part, only those who cared to look—though the magic still danced.

You could make great food, you could cast astonishing spells, but at the end of the day, the wonder of the restaurant came from the people who visited, from the unexpected interactions that arose. It was something that the modern world all too often forgot, the power of a community. That sometimes, it was not a question of being comfortable or happy or of an instant moment of success, but of showing up. At parties, at restaurants, at events. In a world where individuals were born, grew up, lived and grew old isolated from all but a few close friends and family if they were lucky.

Sometimes, no one at all if they weren't.

In the restaurant, though, here in Mo Meng's place of power, some of those barriers lowered. People rejoiced over the foods, savored the tastes and lingered over their meals. They understood, instinctively, that they were safe and protected. Not just from the hazards and threats of the world outside, but also the slings and stones of condemnation.

Forced to interact with one another, pushed to sit with those they might have disliked or hated or had a grudge against—real or –imagined—they did that one thing that so many had forgotten. They talked. Interacted and bonded over a shared, transcendental experience in the meal –itself—or the occasional serving snafu.

After all, for all her skill, for all her hurried movements, Mo Meng had been alone for a time till

Kelly came along. Even now, with added help from Damian, she was stretched ‑thin—forced to hurry between seated patrons, those waiting for a table, and the checks that had to be cleared out.

It also didn't help that sometimes, what was acceptable currency for the restaurant was complicated.

"No, we can't take three favors on Tuesday in lieu of the bill," Kelly said, voice patient if a little strained. "You know the rules. You get one chance to pay another way, then we do Canadian dollars here, paid in cash or by card. No American Express or Diners Club either." She raised a finger and waggled it. "And don't start about how we can avoid more taxes by bartering or letting you have another chance. I like ‑taxes—they pay for my healthcare."

"Well, if not a favor, perhaps these?" The tall, thin figure with ears just a little pointed and amazing skin gestured down, a trio of golden ‑coins—much darker than you'd assume from most movies, due to a higher gold ‑content—appearing on the table. "Much more than the value of a meal. We could put the rest on a tab."

"Cash dollars. Canadian," Kelly said, one foot tapping the ground in impatience. "Non-glamoured. Don't think I won't check." Reaching into her skirt, she pulled out a small rod of cold iron and waved it before the speaker to punctuate her point.

"So rude." On the other hand, the coins disappeared back into the sleeve or pocket or the ether without further complaint. In turn, a non-glamoured credit card appeared. She checked, of course, but there were limits to what magic could do—and dealing with the complicated intricacies of financial exchanges and credit card processing ran right up against them. For one thing, as she understood it, the magic user actually had to understand what they were doing, and the modern financial system, never mind computer code, was outside most of their skillsets.

Payment received, she stepped away to tackle the next problem, a customer coming through the door. She managed to get to him just as he put his foot on the floor, looking all kinds of belligerent. Experienced eyes swept over him, checking ears, fingers, teeth, eyes and waist in quick order for telltale signs and finding nothing. Just as important a clue to his origins was his bearing, the lines on his face and the slight plasticity that came from Botox use adding to the mulish look.

"You said it would be only forty-five minutes. We've been waiting for an hour!" the man growled, drawing himself up so that he could loom over Kelly, his American accent all too clear. New York maybe, or something from the East Coast at least.

"Sorry! I think you might have misheard. I said it was a minimum of forty-five minutes for a table," Kelly replied, meeting glaring brown eyes with her own placid ones.

"I demand to see your manager! This kind of wait is entirely unacceptable."

"I am the manager," Kelly replied. A small lie, but considering there was just Mo Meng and herself till recently and he was even worse at interacting with the public, a reasonable one. "And there is nothing we can do for you at this time. In fact, I believe we might be closing off any further seatings."

"What!? Impossible."

"Quite possible, sir. Today's been particularly busy, and we only have so many servings," Kelly said.

"We came here on our vacation to eat here. We will not leave till we've eaten!" Voice rising now, attracting attention.

Kelly's lips thinned, annoyed. "You can demand, but there's still not going to be food. In fact, you can just leave now."

"What!?"

"Leave," Kelly said. "I'm removing you from the list and banning you."

"What kind of service is that? Have you never heard of the customer is always right?"

"I have. I'm choosing to ignore it."

"You—!" A hand twitched as he stepped closer, but Kelly refused to move. Daring him to take the swing that he obviously wanted to make. She did, however, feel a chill come over her, and watched from close proximity as the man blanched. He stepped back once, and then again, suddenly sweating profusely. "I'm going to leave a bad review for this! On Yelp and Google!"

"Please do." Kelly offered him a cold smile. "It might keep others like you away."

"Well, I never..." Spinning on his heels, he stalked up the stairs to where his companion had watched the entire interaction with a resigned, long-suffering look on her face. Meeting Kelly's eyes, his companion gave the smallest of smiles before the man grabbed her hand and hauled her away.

Jolting to a stop, Kelly looked down to see a hand on her wrist, holding her still. She had not even realized she was moving. She glared at the owner of the hand, intent on being released.

"It's no use. She's chosen her fate," Damian said.

"And what do you know about it?" Kelly snapped.

"Twisted relationships?" A mocking smile traced a line across his face. "Nothing, nothing at all."

Then he was gone, returning to his duties, leaving Kelly frustrated, but unable to do anything. Because he was right—the man's companion hadn't looked like she was ready to leave. And anything she could have said or done would likely just have escalated the situation.

Sometimes, nothing was the hardest thing to do.

Even so, as she came by Ursula and Marilyn's table, she was not surprised to see the older woman look up, answering the question she hadn't had a chance to ask. "I'll watch. Meddle if I have to. I know a few people in Bangor."

"Thankless task," Marilyn pointed out.

"It always is. Dangerous too, but someone has to do it."

"A better person than me." Marilyn tapped the table and the small tablet she'd extracted, a series of scribbled notes on it. "Now, we were talking overages," she continued.

As she slipped away, footsteps just a little lighter, Kelly overheard Ursula mutter under her breath. "Damn lawyers..."

A harsh indictment, but probably fair.

Twenty-Three
Joys of Experimentation

Dessert was always going to be a messy affair. First come, first served, with an every man for himself pursuit of the scarce and varied desserts. Most were older dishes, leftovers from the last couple of days and in some cases weeks, servings that had been overstocked. Magic had kept most of the plates fresh, though some had taken on that twisting taste of magic, that fizz on the tongue and the sweet-sour turning of time magic. A delicacy for some, off-putting for others.

One of the reasons Mo Meng never liked using it. On the other hand, there were only so many desserts he could eat without putting on pounds himself, and at his age, the weight got ever harder to take off. Unfair, really. You would think that magic would help with that, but he had seen the aftereffects of overuse of metabolic magic. Much like cosmetic plastic surgery, it was easy to start—hard to stop.

Of course, Mo Meng was blatantly ignoring the fact that living for literal millennia was also entirely unfair, but that was the useful thing about being human—you could be a hypocrite and selfish and still be a good person, or at least, good enough.

Raiding his fridge and pulling out desserts for his guests was a matter of reaching for the items in the front. He regularly rotated items on the first two levels, mostly to ensure that he always took the oldest items first. In this case, as orders for the end of the meal arrived, whatever dessert he grabbed was what the guests received.

Barring allergies, of course.

Sago with coconut milk and gula malacca, a small batch run when he had been testing a new sago supplier, with colorful tapioca balls infused with a variety of additional tastes. A batch of coffee sago, another made of yam and tapioca, a vanilla-infused concoction—one of his better choices—and two types of tea—green and –black—were all that were left. Some other options, like the durian sago infusion, had been made in single batches and consumed before being vetoed. A personal favorite, perhaps, but not for the general public.

Any sago he sent out, he made sure to pay attention to the reactions of his guests, adding to his storehouse of knowledge of what worked—or not.

Next up were four ramekins of a golden caramel dessert. Crème brulée required a touch of flame at the end to harden and create the caramelized shell it was known for. A chef's butane torch was the perfect tool for that, unless you felt like being fancy. You could set the entire thing alight and do a presentation that way—rum and other proof spirits thrown on the dish, or a small flamethrower rather than a butane torch. Magic, even, if you were into that.

As with so many things, taste and entertainment took a backseat to practicality. In this case, having enough serving staff to take the time to conduct an elaborate presentation—and ensure one's customers didn't accidentally burn themselves on say, a marshmallow you provided to toast over the flames as they waited for the spirits to burn off—was a necessity. One that the restaurant lacked.

Fire flaring to life with a hiss and click, the flame burning tight and blue. He quickly adjusted the knob to reduce the flame to the right level before playing it over the dessert, listening to the hiss and crack, watching sugars melt, bubble and caramelize on the dish. There was something atavistic in utilizing flame like this, just as satisfying as the grill or the gas wok.

Four dishes didn't take long to finish. With a reluctant sigh, Mo Meng put away the torch.

Perhaps he'd run a night full of flame soon.

Next up were tubs of homemade ice cream. You could do a lot with the right mixer, plenty of cream, vanilla and patience. Like tapioca, homemade ice cream also had the advantage of letting you experiment with various flavor profiles without committing to a large amount of work.

In this case, there were a half-dozen flavors remaining after unleashing the experiments on Kelly and himself, and now, on his paying customers. Mostly the regulars, he hoped; but you never knew who might receive what—which was the thrill of today.

Some of the flavors were prosaic—using a different kind of orange to create the extract or a new farm for his strawberries—while others were more of an attempt at replicating a specific taste. Carbonara fettucine, oyster, applewood, a spring rainbow and the first winter snow.

Conceptual or weird, but that was what kept –life—and cooking—interesting.

After that, well, he had a bunch of more boring types of desserts. Chocolate mousses, slices of cake—two types of chocolate decadence, red velvet and berry explosion cakes—a mango pudding dessert topped with real mango slices and red sesame balls. Even some traditional fried red bean dessert pancakes.

When he hit the back of the fridge with a half-dozen orders still left, even he was surprised.

"What is this?" Damian asked, helping Kelly pick up the plates of dessert that she had directed him to. The berry explosion cake was self-evident, but the pair of ice creams and the dark green tapioca balls from the sago were a little more confusing.

"Experiments. Pretty sure the sago is green tea," Kelly said, waving at him to hurry up. Everyone was rushing the pair now, now that the food had run out and last call had come. Otherwise she'd have handled it herself. "He keeps trying those with his friend, swearing he'll get them right at some point. They've tried a half-dozen different tea blends, but they always come out either too tea-like or so subtle that the gula malacca washes out the flavor."

"And the ice cream?" Damian sniffed a little, surreptitiously, trying to discern the smells coming off it. One was familiar, but not what he would have expected for an ice cream. What kind of over-enthusiastic health junkie had come up with that idea?

"Don't know. We'll find out," Kelly said brightly, as she arrived at the family's table. The four hyter sprites were diluted blood supernaturals, their mixed sprite and human heritage barely more than a nod towards their origins, a particularly long nose reminiscent of a beak, the way their hair slicked back like tufts of feathers, subconscious folding of hands at their sides like wings.

It still left the family in an uncomfortable place, caught between two worlds and not truly of either, struggling for acceptance from both sides of the world. She felt for them, knowing how hard it was to survive caught between the seen and unseen, between two disparate cultures. Always questioning where you belonged. She felt for them, being in the same situation herself nowadays.

Was it a surprise that a large percentage of those involved either went full mundane or joined DESE as agents and administrative staff? At least, that way, they had a job and people who understood.

"Four desserts, random choice. We have a previous day's dessert special, the berry explosion filled with local raspberries, strawberries and blueberries and organic cream on a gluten free flour base, and three sets of the Mo Meng special."

"What's so special?" the teenager of the group asked, pulling his head out of his handheld computer game to stare suspiciously at the plates the servers held.

"Special because he was experimenting. These were small batches that might or more likely, might not ever, make it to the menu."

"So they're bad."

Kelly smiled, refusing to answer.

"I'll take the orange one!" the youngest girl, barely more than a toddler, cried out. "It's the same color as my dress!"

Damian put the plate of bright orange ice cream down in front of the girl, then at the mom's gesture deposited the cake in front of her. The father asked for the sago, leaving the too slow teenage boy to receive the last bowl of brown-colored ice cream.

"That isn't coffee, is it?" the father muttered out of the side of his mouth to Kelly, eyeing the unfortunately tinted dessert.

"No, definitely not coffee or caffeine related," she said. "Yours is, though."

"That's fine..." the dad smiled.

"This is edible, right?" the teenager asked, suspiciously.

"Mo Meng himself has tested all the dishes here," Kelly said brightly. "Happy eating."

Then with a wave, she had Damian backing off, a little glint of humor in her eyes.

"That's a meat-infused and carrot pair of ice creams, right?" he whispered once they were sufficiently far away.

"Carrot and beef Wellington, yes."

"And they say my father is mad."

Dinner service was ending. Mo Meng turned off the grills and cleaned up the last dregs of food, plating them to go out to the remaining customers who had stuck around long enough to receive seats. As he did so, he watched the reaction to his experiments.

He was a bit gleeful about doing this, for the process of introducing new dishes was always a thrill. You never knew how someone would react to a new taste. Back in the old days, it was as simple as bringing one cuisine to another region, but these days it required more experimentation and effort as international cuisines and ingredients made their way around the world. Experimentation, effort, creativity, and a gleeful disregard for the sensibilities of the common people were the hallmarks of a new dish. Or element in a dish.

"This is so wrong..." the teenager was whisper-shouting as he struggled with his need to voice his concern and feelings while battling a teenager's natural insecurity. All the while, his spoon never stopped moving, scraping pieces off the beef Wellington infused ice cream.

Mo Meng was rather proud of that creation.

It had required multiple attempts, most of them involving infusion of warmed heavy cream with beef drippings, such that the flavor held through the creaming and freezing process. The heavy fat, already flavored by the beef Wellington, boosted the signature taste, while the crunchiness of small pieces of bread helped give it a further textural authenticity. Of course, he had to flash-freeze the bread so that it would not soften and dampen before it was mixed in. All in all, it was a creation that he was about ninety-five percent certain had achieved his desired result—an ice cream that tasted and felt like beef Wellington.

Whether that was a desirable end result... well. Sometimes, you asked if you could, and then did it before you asked if you should. A fair decision-making methodology when it came to cooking. Not so much with magic or atomic bombs.

"Can't be that wrong. You can't stop eating it. Let me try some." The father made grabby hands, only for the boy to hunch over his ice cream possessively.

"You going to share too?" the boy asked.

"Of course not." Looking affronted, the father continued, "Now, gimme!"

At the same time, the mother was watching with amusement as her daughter polished off the last of the carrot ice cream, looked her mother straight in the eyes and defiantly said, "Make carrot ice cream and I promise to eat it."

Sometimes, all you had to do to trick others into eating your creations was add a lot of sugar and salt.

Twenty-Four
Final Numbers

T he pair of contestants pushed up with a groan of concentrated effort, glaring at one another and neither willing to concede defeat. Their weapons of war were laid low, the spoils stolen and consumed. Only the remnants, the discarded terrain of battle, remained in the tottering towers of plates beside each contestant. Sitting beside the pair, silent in quiet and horrified admiration, were the pair of DESE agents.

"Mine's taller."

"Only because you have a thicker plate there!" Tobias jabbed a finger forward and pointed two-thirds of the way down. "And there." Again the finger shifted. "We have the exact same number of plates! Twenty-three each."

"Exact same number, yes? So you agree that is true?" Jotun replied.

Sensing a trap, Tobias hesitated but had to agree.

"Ah, but I stole the contents of one of yours," Jotun crowed. "I finished all of your fried chicken, do you not recall?"

"You, but, the plate..." Had been added to his own pile. Defeated, Tobias slumped, his body sagging. Only to bounce back up, raising a finger. "I can order another plate."

"No, you cannot." Kelly appeared beside the pair, hands on her hips. "We're out. And we're not reopening the kitchen. It's time to pay up." A pair of bills landed in front of each of them with a satisfying thump.

"Of course." Jotun smirked, reached for the bill and pushed it towards the wincing Mika. O sitting beside him was shaking her head, obviously imagining the upcoming discussion with accounting about the expense claim. Tobias grinned, copying the motion as Mika nodded at Kelly.

"Don't forget to tip well!" Tobias pointed out to Mika as he took the card machine from Kelly.

"Always do," Mika said, with a lopsided grin. "It's not as though it's my money."

"More ours," grumbled Jotun, arms crossed. "Damn supernatural tax..."

"Tell me about it," Tobias said. "Do you know, they started leveling a new tax on our steel? Something about unfair competing practices, using natural lava flows as our fuel source or something. As though the humans don't get subsidies on their oil!"

The pair stood up, nodding perfunctory thanks to the pair of DESE agents before exiting, complaining to one another about taxes, their earlier competition and bet forgotten. Kelly wondered if they'd ever remember to set the conditions of winning, or if it was just one of those 'favors' that the supernatural enjoyed trading.

Either way, the pair were careful to waddle out gingerly, surreptitiously clutching their stomachs as they left. Moments later, O and Mika made their exit too, the female agent staring suspiciously at Damian and the ladies. She bent low to whisper, Kelly catching something about even more paperwork to file before they passed out of earshot.

As always, she made sure to forget what she overheard. It was none of her business, any of it. As the saying went, not her monkeys, not her circus.

"Well, that's them then." Picking up the glasses and the bill containers, she wondered how much longer Marilyn and the Professor were going to be here. They had been fighting over a glowing tablet, reading and adding minor textual changes throughout the meal. They had been so focused, they'd almost forgotten to order dessert and would have lost out, if not for Damian. Now the boy was hovering beside them, looking frustrated and impatient at the same time.

"Well?" he asked.

"It's good. Now you'll just have to read it over," Marilyn replied.

"You read it over, what's wrong with it?"

"Nothing. Not anymore. You should still take the time to read it again and think over the deal before signing."

"I already thought about it. I don't need to rethink it."

"He has," Ursula said. "He's a big boy, let him sign. These old bones don't like staying out so long."

"No." Marilyn closed the tablet with a snap, the glow shutting off immediately. "As my client, I'm advising you to take a moment." She tapped the now closed case. "The contract is binding no matter time or distance, so a little delay will not matter."

A broad smile appeared on the older woman's face, the Professor leaning forward as her voice dropped. "Except to the enchantments in the restaurant." Unlike some of their other visitors, the professor lacked the quiet danger, that sense of unease the others engendered. It was, perhaps, why Kelly found herself even more wary of the woman.

Her boss appeared, having come over with nary a sound, startling Damian who swore under his breath and then ducked his head in embarrassment. Not that she blamed him; Mo Meng could move like a ninja when he wanted. Even if that was culturally inappropriate.

"My enchantments will hold," Mo Meng said.

"And those outside? Are you taking responsibility for what happens once he is uncontained?"

"You know I've sworn off that." His words caused the professor to whip around to stare directly at her boss, surprise registering on that lined face. "As a matter of phrasing, not literally."

"Oh! Good." She patted the place over her heart. "Sometimes you worry me."

"Absolute statements have a tendency to be turned upon one, the longer you live."

"Amen to that," Marilyn echoed. "Which is why you should be careful with this contract. The entire contract is time limited with an automatic extension that expires after three renewals, but still, you never know what you'll regret."

"Though binding yourself properly can give more power," Ursula said. "Ask old One-eye."

"It's not power he needs. Just control," Mo Meng corrected. "And I'll ask you not to invoke him in my place of business."

"I thought you'd put to bed your old grudge," the professor said.

"We did. I'm more annoyed by what he's letting them do with his pantheon," Mo Meng said.

"Well, you know he'd say he's limited..."

"That's..." Now he hesitated, looking over at the three who were watching the pair argue with bated breath. He snorted and pointed at the tablet. "Take your time. And be careful about what's promised. What seems like a good deal might not be, given time. Permanent sacrifices for temporary gains is rarely a good deal."

"Fine." Damian rolled his eyes and snatched the tablet from him. "Really, you olds are just... ugh!"

The group watched the boy stalk away before turning to one another, Marilyn the one to break the silence. "Olds? Certainly not! I haven't even hit my first millennium."

Ursula reached over and patted the other woman's hand. "And you don't look a day over three centuries."

"You hag—!"

Having scored the final point, Ursula dropped a handful of crumpled bills extracted from her purse onto the table. She leaned in to whisper something to Mo Meng just before she left, leaving him looking bemused.

Kelly picked up the bills, eyeballing the amount while the older woman was still making her way out of the restaurant. You never knew who might stiff you.

Though you could almost always tell who the bad tippers would be. Church groups after Sunday service to start with, which was one reason she was grateful Mo Meng never worked Sundays or lunch hours. Clout chasers were another, as well as the occasional Bay Street bros. She doubted she could handle them, not after working here.

In short order, even Marilyn had paid her bill—a sleek, faceless black card in her case—leaving Kelly alone to admire the tables that were already half-cleaned. Damian had a spray bottle in one hand and a fresh cloth in the other, wiping each down in quick order. Once he was done, they'd have to put the chairs up to give the floor a proper sweep and mop, but that was a job for later.

Right now…

"You save me any?" she said, eyes fixed on her boss.

"Save you what?"

"The desserts, of course." She bounced on her toes to get some blood flow going and relieve the mild ache from being on her feet for hours on end.

"Yes. One of the better successes, I think." He said that as he left to return to the kitchen.

"Don't tell me that." She pouted. "The surprise is half the fun."

"You didn't say that when I made the chili and mango and stewed pork brownie."

A slight shudder showed what she thought of that dish. It should have had the right flavor profiles, just like pineapple in curry. Except that the addition of the stewed pork and the sweetness of mango without the tartness of pineapple, along with the gummy, floury consistency of the brownie, had left it cloying rather than tasty. Also strangely edible, in the 'I hate myself for liking this' way that black licorice could create.

The thump of a bowl brought her back to the present and she found herself seated by the counter, already drooling at the sight. Ice cream, pale but not white, a slight yellowish tinge to it. She further noted small chunks of yellow in it, golden pieces that glittered a little.

Using the provided spoon, she cut into the all too soft ice cream. Without additional preservatives, the ice cream had begun to melt almost immediately after being removed from the freezer, though only a mild sheen covered the single—if generous—scoop that lay on the rectangular plate before her.

Pushing down, she watched as the spoon cut through with ease, a generous dollop rising to her lips. She sniffed a little, wrinkling her nose at the smell, trying to place it but failing. It was a familiar scent, though she wondered why she could not recall it before she placed the spoon between her lips, feeling the ice cream slide down onto her tongue.

Cold, enough to make her curl her tongue, was the first sensation. Then, taste registered the sweetness in the cream, the slight acidity that married with the sweetness. She recognized the smell now, the taste as it permeated her mouth—apples. Except, of course, there was a slight tingle in her mouth, in the back of her throat as she bit down and then chewed, finding a hardened piece of golden loveliness. She bit down with a crunch, intense sweetness exploding in her mouth as it mixed with the heavy cream and vanilla and tartness of the dish.

Then it was gone, and she was onto the next scoop and the next, forgetting for a time her aching feet, the additional work left to do and the counting of tips. Just enjoying, for a moment, a dish that was unexpected and lovely.

"Apple juice and that was honeycomb, wasn't it?" Kelly asked when she was done.

"Not exactly."

"You're right. It was too tart, too sharp for apple juice. But it was apple, right?" A nod confirmed her guess. "Then, apple cider?" The small smile of acknowledgment made her shake her head. "Alcoholic ice cream isn't exactly new, though the honeycomb was a nice touch."

Mo Meng shrugged. "There are more experimenters than there are me, nor do I claim to be at the forefront of my craft. As Lily would say, I'm more of a workhorse, following after the trailblazers. I'll never make anything truly new, but I do try to keep up."

"I don't know about that..." Kelly looked back as Damian worked diligently, silently, only looking up once in a while to stare at the closet where he had secreted the tablet. "Maybe what you make is just a little harder to categorize."

"Alcoholic ice cream isn't hard to categorize. Just look under 'ways to add alcohol to everything'."

"Well, I think it's great. You should make it again. Or something like it," Kelly said, bouncing to her feet, the soreness gone. "And maybe more carrot ice cream. We can con our guests into eating healthier."

Laughing softly, Mo Meng waved her off. Like her, he had a lot more work to do before the restaurant was ready to close. If nothing else, since his newest employee had not burned his restaurant down or cursed a customer to hell, he had paperwork to fill in.

Death, taxes, and magic, all of it persisted from age to age.

The End

Thank you for reading Thaumaturgic Tapas! Want to return to the Nameless Restaurant right away? Visit www.mylifemytao.com/bonus-epilogues/ to read a short scene set after this book. Mo Meng will be back in Sorcerous Plates.

Author's Note

The eagle eyed among you might have noticed that the name of the book changed somewhere in the middle of the year. That was because I had been busy working on recipes and the book itself, and both ran together to push the work into a series of dishes with smaller plates, rather than my initial concept.

While I do all of the recipes that show up in the Hidden Dishes universe, only a few make their way into regular rotation at home. There are reasons for that, chief amongst them the degree of fondness for the dish at home and ease of production. Some items - like the satay and other kebabs - require the BBQ which is available only half the year. Others, like the garlic smashed potatoes, are simple enough to do and a major hit.

Of course, the French Onion Soup takes forever;

but during winter months can be a sweet and cold comfort. Utilizing a second pair of hands - the spawn - to deal with the many, many onions also helps matters, though the need for broth can be a major limiting factor. Unlike Mo Meng though, I can - and will - cheat; utilizing both store-bought broth and mixed bone broth. The taste might be muddied a little, but it's still warm and comforting.

Which is perhaps how I would describe this series and its place in my writing calendar. Not challenging per se; but warm and comforting. A mental hug to my creative juices, as I struggle through more complex world building tasks in my other work.

I hope you enjoyed the novella and will continue on with me. While there's no major, world-shaking events happening; I do have an 'end' plot in mind for this series which should happen in another 3-4 novellas.

~Tao

About the Author

Tao Wong is a Canadian author based in Toronto who is best known for his System Apocalypse post-apocalyptic LitRPG series and A Thousand Li, a Chinese xianxia fantasy series. His work has been released in audio, paperback, hardcover and ebook formats and translated into German, Spanish, Portuguese, Russian and other languages. He was shortlisted for the UK Kindle Storyteller award in 2021 for his work, A Thousand Li: the Second Sect. When he's not writing and working, he's practicing martial arts, reading and dreaming up new worlds.

Tao became a full-time author in 2019 and is a member of SF Canada, the Science Fiction and Fantasy Writers of America (SFWA) and ALLI.

For updates on the series and his other books (and special one-shot stories), please visit the author's website: http://www.mylifemytao.com

Subscribe to Tao's mailing list to receive exclusive access to short stories in the Thousand Li and System Apocalypse universes.

If you'd like to support Tao directly, he has a Patreon page - benefits include previews of all his new books, full access to series short stories, and other exclusive perks. Tao Wong Patreon

Or visit Tao's Facebook Page: www.facebook.com/taowongauthor/

Tao also hosts a Facebook Group for all things cultivation novels. We'd love it if you joined us: Cultivation Novels

For more great information about LitRPG series, check out the Facebook groups:

- GameLit Society

- LitRPG Books

- LitRPG Legion

About the Publisher

Starlit Publishing is wholly owned and operated by Tao Wong. It is a science fiction and fantasy publisher focused on the LitRPG & cultivation genres. Their focus is on promoting new, upcoming authors in the genre whose writing challenges the existing stereotypes while giving a rip-roaring good read.

For more information on Starlit Publishing, visit our website!

You can also join Starlit Publishing's mailing list to learn of new, exciting authors and book releases.